THE DOOR OF
TIRELESS PURSUIT

ALSO BY STEPHEN T. VESSELS

The Mountain & The Vortex and Other Tales

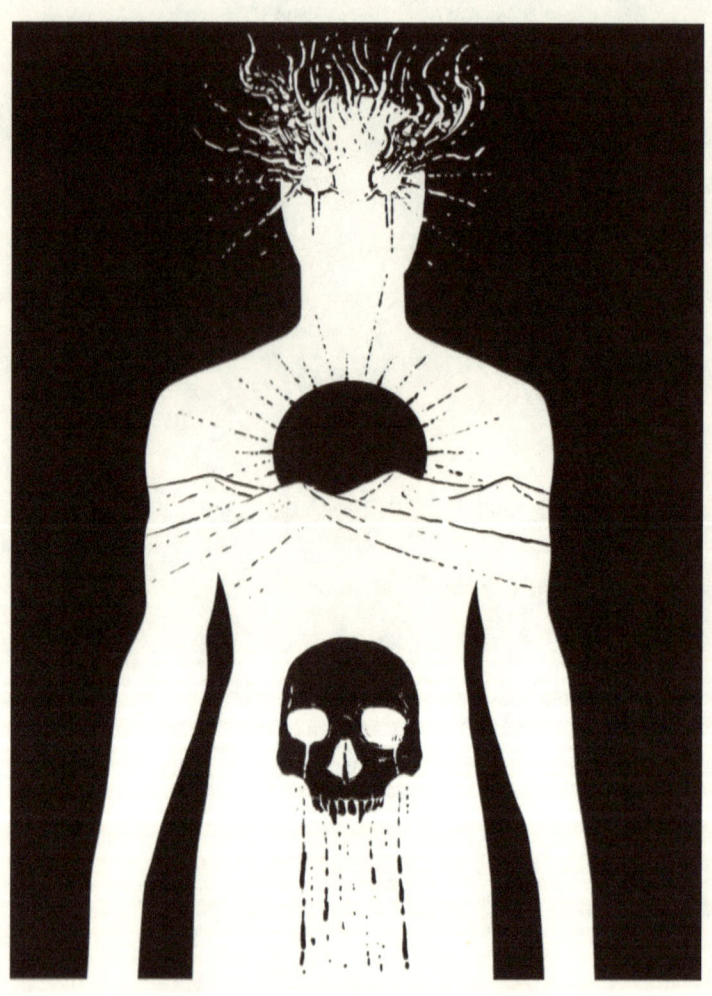

THE DOOR OF TIRELESS PURSUIT

A LABYRINTH OF SOULS NOVEL

BY

STEPHEN T. VESSELS

ShadowSpinners Press

Cover art by Josephe Vandel.
Book design by Matthew Lowes.

ShadowSpinners Press
shadowspinnerspress.com

Typeset in
Minion Pro by Robert Slimbach
and IM FELL Double Pica by Igino Marini.
The Fell Types are digitally reproduced
by Igino Marini, www.iginomarini.com.

Learn more about
the Labyrinth of Souls game at
matthewlowes.com/games.

for Robin Burrows

ACKNOWLEDGEMENTS

Thanks to Christina Lay and Matthew Lowes for creating opportunities and doing the heavy lifting; to Elizabeth Engstrom for having a brilliant thought and inviting me into the fold; to John R. Reed, and again, Liz and Christina, for their invaluable assistance refining the tale; to Oja Fin for reading and responding at the drop of a hat; to Rick Shaw, Nicholas Deitch, Mac Talley, Maryanne Knight, Christine Logsdon, Hector Javkin, Sid Stebel, Karen Ford, Linda Chase, Dyanne Asimov, Ted Humphrey, and Andrew Loschert for listening carefully and responding thoughtfully; to Ian Wood and L. Λ. Howe for always being there and believing; and to Chloé McFeters for being my personal angel and guiding light. Special appreciation to Chris Wozny for her ardent and indefatigable support, and for being the best editor I ever had.

Editor's Preface

Dungeon Solitaire: Labyrinth of Souls is a fantasy game for tarot cards, written by Matthew Lowes and Illustrated by Josephe Vandel. In the game you defeat monsters, disarm traps, open doors, and explore mazes as you delve the depths of a dangerous dungeon. Along the way you collect treasure and magic items, gain skills, and gather companions.

Now ShadowSpinners Press is publishing this and other stand-alone novels inspired by the game. Each *Labyrinth of Souls* novel features a journey into a unique vision of the underworld.

The Labyrinth of Souls is more than an ancient ruin filled with monsters, trapped treasure, and the lost tombs of bygone kings. It is a manifestation of a mythic underworld, existing at a crossroads between people and cultures, between time and space, between the physical world and the deepest reaches of the psyche. It is a dark mirror held up to human experience, in which you may find your dreams ... or your doom. Entrances to this realm can appear in any time period, in any location. There are innumerable reasons why a person may enter, but it is a place antagonistic to those who do, a place where monsters dwell, with obstacles and illusions to waylay adventurers, and whose very walls can be a force of corruption. It is a haunted place, ever at the edge of sanity.

THE DOOR OF
TIRELESS PURSUIT

PART ONE

THE SCHOOL OF A THOUSAND DREAMS

CHAPTER ONE

Alexander had just decided that the mall was the wrong place to look for a replacement for his missing vernier caliper when he saw the woman who would change his life. He took her in all at once, the way a grown man can a woman who calls to all that he is, from his callouses to his boyhood soul: starburst eyes, flowing red hair, lithe body in a breezy dress; high cheekbones, softly pronounced; jaw-line smooth as a chalice; a kind, intelligent brow; strong, even nose; melodious lips, round chin raised to meet the moment—a fortuitous conjunction of ancestry harboring a bright and stalwart spirit. If she hadn't looked at him he would have gone by wishing he were younger and remembered her in his fantasies.

But she did look at him, and kept looking, and as she drew near an unreasonable hope roused in him. Electric Light Orchestra's "Summer and Lightning" played on the mall sound system like a chance serenade.

At the exact moment when he might have failed himself and moved on, he feigned confusion. "Do you know how to get out of here?"

She smirked in an amiable way. "In a hurry are you?" She stopped in front of him and they became an obstacle in the cross-flow of shoppers.

"Not … really." He laughed evasively. "But this place is a maze."

She drew so close he could feel her breath. His mind stalled. She smelled of peonies and pepper, looked up at him like a yearning child, with that in her eyes which spoke of aeons.

"My God you're beautiful," he said, unaware of speaking aloud. He lifted his hand to touch her face but stopped himself. She brought her hand close to his and an electric spark passed between them. He gasped. She brushed her fingertips against his and her lips parted. He saw her burning heart, wrapped in thorns. Alexander became someone he'd never been, seized her in his arms and kissed her. Holy Mother of Jesus, she kissed him back.

Some blissful eternity later they released each other. She mouthed *"Wow,"* and he could only stare.

Still without thinking, he said, "I love you."

They stood a moment in awkward silence. He had no idea what to say.

"Are you really lost?" she asked.

He opened his mouth, closed it, shook his head. "More like found, I think." *I hope.*

Her gaze slid right. "Well, there's an exit there."

He looked down the overbright, ersatz spectacle of the mall, and registered the row of glass doors, leading out. "Oh," he said.

She wove her arm around his. "Take me away from here."

He didn't care about anything he'd cared about a moment before. "Your wish is my command."

Her laughter was the most beautiful sound he'd ever heard. He could live his whole life and pine for no better music. They walked toward the doors.

Now he was truly lost, and scared. He didn't know what to say or do, and dreaded blowing it with this fey creature. She couldn't really be interested in him. He must be a plaything to her, a momentary diversion in a day driven by willful pursuits.

He remembered the look in her eyes after they kissed, the joy and release in her laughter, and it seemed true, and that he was not deceiving himself. He could think of no better way to expend his life than find out.

They stepped outside and Sandy became disoriented. Tall brick buildings surrounded a park bordered by broad thoroughfares bustling with traffic. This wasn't Los Angeles; it looked more like New York.

He stared about in bewilderment. "Where are we?"

She turned him to face her. "Where do you want to be?"

He swallowed and tried to think, but the only answer in his head was, "With you."

"Then roll with it, okay?"

He nodded, having no idea what he was agreeing to.

She studied him, tilting her head, smiled, as if some instinct she possessed were confirmed. "Come on. I know a place."

He let her lead him along the street, weaving through the mill of pedestrians. They crossed an intersection and she took him down a side street.

"Wait." He stopped. "Tell me what's going on."

She took her time answering, appraising him further. "What's your name?"

He blinked at her. "Sandy. Alexander—my friends call me Sandy."

"Sandy, I'm Quints, and *my* friends call me Lark." She held his face in her hands. "I didn't pick you and you didn't pick me. We found each other, understand?"

He shook his head.

She placed her hand on his heart. "Stop thinking; just feel. You said you love me. Did you mean it?"

He swallowed. "Yes." Looking in her eyes it still felt true; spontaneous emotion had become balled up in confusion. Again, though, it was the only answer his mind made room for.

Again with that smile. "Good. I know it seems impossible but I love you too. And right now I want you to trust me. Can you do that?"

Changes took place in his body, mind and being he could never have named. All he had to say was 'yes,' and so he squared up and said it like a prayer.

"Wow," she said, this time out loud.

He wanted to make her laugh again, so he made a face and she did and he stopped caring where he was or what made sense or how the world was meant to be.

She led him down to a subway station and they boarded a train. They sat down and she snuggled against him, and he felt suffused by holy grace, and all uncertainty about the immediate course of his life was vanquished. He nevertheless stared about in continued bewilderment.

"This is New York, isn't it?" He felt her head nod against his chest. He'd told her he would trust her, so he did, and set aside needing to understand, yielding to the ameliorating confirmation of a childhood belief, never fully relinquished, that magic existed, and the world was more than it seemed.

They reached a stop and he followed her back up to the street. They seemed to be somewhere in Chinatown.

Past another series of turns through streets redolent of fish, herbs and refuse she led him down a narrow flight of stairs to a red door.

"Let me do the talking," she said.

He shrugged. He'd never been so bereft of words in his life.

She knocked; a slot in the door opened and eyes peered out.

"Ramshackle," Lark said.

The eyes fixed on Sandy. "Who's he?"

"Knight-errant," she answered.

The peephole closed and the door opened.

They entered a dark bar crowded with the most varied assortment of people Sandy had ever seen in one place. Every race and age, from adolescent to elderly, seemed represented, dressed in manners outlandish and ordinary. She led him through a warren of rooms, wending through the crowd and between tables, here and there exchanging greetings with people she knew. Sandy endured a series of curious looks.

The last room was centered by an uplit mirror pool. Lark led him to an open, red-leather moon booth on the far side of the pool.

A waiter came.

"Gin fizz," Lark said.

Sandy puffed out a breath. "Have any single malt Scotch?"

The waiter, a tall, slim person with skin the color of espresso and the features of Adonis, said, "Certainly," in a mellifluous, tenor voice. "Name your preference, sir. Our selection is quite substantial."

Sandy was too dazed to be skeptical. "Jura, Durach's Own."

The waiter withdrew and Sandy let himself relax in Lark's gaze. She knew what he wanted to know and would explain when she was ready.

"We quickened," she said.

He waited for her to go on.

"Not many people can do it. You're one of the few."

He waited for her to say more. When she didn't, he said, "You know that doesn't … quite serve as an explanation."

She laughed. "I can't explain it, not really. But you can look at it like this: There's the physical way to travel, on foot or in a car, but there's another way that is invisible to most people, even though, really, they do it all the time."

"I have never done … *that*."

She laughed again. "But you just *did*, and that means you can. It's in the relationship between time and space, which most people don't understand. 'Now' isn't just gone before you know it, it doesn't exist. There's no such thing as a moment. Everything is one, continuous flow. Every time you make a choice, turn right or left, stay up or go to bed, you change the course of your life, and go someplace new.

"Most people only choose courses that go where they expect. Whenever you take a risk, the entire landscape of your reality changes. When you kissed me, you let go of knowing where your action would take you. You entered another landscape."

Nothing she said made sense, but he enjoyed hearing her say it. Then again maybe it did, and it had just been a long time since he'd let himself think that way, maybe not since childhood. He'd entered a detached state in which he didn't much care about any of it. He just wanted to be close to her. The only mystery he cared about solving was her.

"So why did you bring me here?"

"It's a place where the Quick come. You're one of us, now. I mean, you can be. And I thought you might want a drink."

"Really?"

She was startled.

"You think the thing I'm most interested in right now is a drink?"

Her expression changed to amusement and they weren't in a bar anymore but a bedroom. Not a room but a place among the stars. Five pairs of curtains, four open, one closed, hung on walls that weren't there. Star fields and galaxies and rogue planets drifted all about them. The floor was carpeted with thick, cool grass. Sandy stared about in wonder until his eyes again found Lark's. Nothing in the universe could compete with her.

She turned and presented her back to him. Sandy unzipped her dress and she let it slip to the floor, faced him. All the saints and Troubadours couldn't have done justice to her beauty. She helped him out of his clothes and lifted her hand, palm out. Sandy stepped close, brushed his fingertips against hers. They smiled and fell together into bed, a domain of softness beneath a bower of emerald vines that seemed to grow from the firmament. Alexander had never made love like that, without any thought for himself. He just wanted her to keep having orgasms. He wanted her whole life to be one, long orgasm.

When he was lying back in the relaxed afterglow of a greater ecstasy than he had ever known, she knelt beside him and they talked in a random, easy way, and he made her laugh. Only starlight lit their love nest, and yet Lark glowed, suffused with pale fire, and he thought that she must be an angel. Never in his life had Sandy felt so completely at home, so certain that he was exactly where and with whom he belonged. He basked in the miracle of her presence as one healed of all wounds, absolved of all sins, made whole and certain upon his path without in any way knowing what path it was.

"What do you do?" she asked.

"You mean for a job? It isn't interesting."

"Tell me anyway."

"I sort bones."

She frowned at him, still smiling, the peaks of her eyebrows twin flames.

"I categorize and catalogue fossils."

"You're a paleontologist."

"Just an assistant. They plop big trays of bones in front of me, and I classify and catalogue them."

"And you're good at it."

He shrugged. "They trust me to get it right. Sometimes I test them—mix things up, see if I can get them to think they've discovered a new species."

She laughed. "Has it worked?"

"They catch on. They know to watch out for me, now. But once in a while. We had this Norwegian guy—no sense of humor, gullible as they come. I had fun with him."

She laughed again. "You're mean."

"Me? I'm a pussycat. Everyone needs a laugh."

They lapsed into a relaxed silence, smiling at each other in the dimness.

She slapped her knees. "You didn't get to finish your drink!"

"I didn't get to *start* it."

"Neither did I, and it was *your* fault. Come on." She jumped off the bed and threw his clothes at him.

They dressed and were back at their table. The slim, black waiter with the face out of Greek mythology arrived with their drinks.

"Jura, sixteen year," he said, placing a glass in front of Sandy, and, "Gin fizz," placing a tall, tubular cocktail in front of Lark.

Sandy sipped the Scotch and nodded approvingly. When the waiter left he said, "Perfect timing. Slow service, though."

"I tweaked time a little."

Sandy lowered his eyes at her. "You … tweaked … time."

She held her finger to her lips, grinning slyly. "So he wouldn't notice we'd left. It's against the rules to quicken in or out of the bar. My membership would be revoked. Well, maybe not *mine,* but Appox would have thrown *you* out …"

Abruptly, her expression went flat. Something in the atmosphere changed. Lark looked at someone across the room, a winsome allure sparking in her eyes.

Sandy tracked the course of her gaze and found their object, a dark-haired man in a long black coat embroidered in black filigree that shone in the light.

Sandy knew he shouldn't do it. Deep inside, a tiny voice warned him. Everything between him and this miraculous woman had happened by mutual accord. He'd been so famished for closeness—more than he'd known—that he didn't listen. He overrode his inner wisdom and pulled her to him. "Hey, you're with me, remember?"

She stiffened. "What makes you think you have the right to treat me like a possession?" She sounded like a petulant child.

"Nothing!" he swore, and drew away, scalded. He looked at nothing, cleared his throat and swallowed, snuck a glance at her and found her doing the same at him—like a frightened child, now.

The man Lark had been fixed on came around the mirror pool to their table and grinned down at her. The embroidery in his coat glimmered with hints of color. "Hello, princess," he said.

Sandy became aware with climbing alarm that every eye in the place was on them. The waiter re-appeared at the entrance to the adjoining room, glowering at the man in the black coat. "Garritch!" he called, in a forbidding tone.

The dark-haired man glanced back. "Appox," he said.

"It is against the rules to quicken into this place."

The man in the black coat chuckled. "Rules." He returned his attention to Lark, who met his gaze with something akin to lust. "We don't obey rules, do we?"

In his raw state the barrier Sandy felt between Lark and him made every second fresh misery. But he registered something else in her eyes: a trance-like glaze. He realized the man in the black coat was doing something to her. A force emanated from the man the waiter called Garritch, flowing past Sandy, like wind outside a window. For a flickering instant he saw it, a hail of tiny arrows, aimed straight at Lark. They fizzled into vapor before hitting her, encountering an invisible barrier. The barrier was wavering.

"Garritch!" the waiter shouted, "you will not cast inside this club! Your membership is re*voked!*"

Anger welled up, in complete abrogation of fear. "Hey!" Sandy shouted, and jumped to his feet. "Deal with *me!*" He hadn't known that *voice* existed in him.

Garritch frowned at him as one might an annoyance. He raised his hand, not to strike but to do something else. Then he sort of oscillated as a gunshot rang out. He turned, sneering, to the waiter, who held a smoking revolver aimed at him. Garritch swung his arm forward. The waiter dodged left; people in the next room were knocked from their chairs and thrown to the floor. The waiter fired again, and this time hit Garritch. Aside from rocking him back a step, it seemed to have little effect. Garritch thrust his hand outward, and an invisible force sliced across the mirror pool, splitting the water in a dual spray. The waiter was thrown back and pinned against the far wall.

Other patrons fled the room or ducked under tables. Sandy slugged Garritch, putting his body into it. The look he got for that was more than annoyance. Before Garritch could react, though, Lark uttered a cry.

She was bleeding from a wound in her chest. The trance had broken, and she looked to Sandy with a desperate appeal.

"No!" Garritch shrieked, and swept in beside her. She tried to push him away but he seized her in his arms and they vanished.

Sandy stared at the empty space where Lark had been. There was a bloody hole in the leather where a bullet had passed through her. The understanding that he could not follow her wherever she had gone seared through him.

The waiter came over, shaken and grim. "I am sorry, sir," he said, "I must ask you to leave. No guest may remain in the club unaccompanied by a mem—"

"You shot her!" Sandy roared, and lunged at the waiter, bearing him to the floor and punching him. Other hands pulled him up and immobilized him.

The waiter got to his feet, rubbing his jaw. "Let him go," he told the others.

Sandy shrugged off the hands that held him, glared at Appox.

"I'm sorry that your visit to the club has been unpleasant. Nevertheless, I must insist that you leave."

The waiter and his fellows escorted Sandy back through the bar to the entrance. Two of Appox's men shoved Sandy outside and closed the door. With the click of its latch, Sandy found himself back inside the Pacific Crest Mall in Santa Monica, in the exact place where he had first taken Lark in his arms and kissed her.

CHAPTER TWO

Alexander drifted to a children's play area, sank onto a plastic bench, vacantly watched shoppers mill back and forth. He couldn't read their minds but he could see them think, all looking for something, diverting themselves from the vagaries of existence, teasing themselves with ephemeral delights. The mall was a kind of school, it struck him, a school of a thousand dreams, all elusive, malformed and unattainable; the shoppers all teaching each other, by mutual pursuit, to keep searching, now and then stopping to blink and gaze about in confusion, caught on the precipice of a terrifying awareness that none of it mattered at all.

Sandy saw Lark's beatific face, alight with pale fire, gazing down at him with the fullness of love, and he wept. He wept inconsolably; playing children and passersby stopped to watch him. He felt their consternation and empathy, how exposed he was, and fled.

He found his car and drove home, at a loss for where else to go. His apartment: a frail shelter for the aims of his heart. Everything neat and orderly, the bed always made, the galley kitchen always clean, the only disarray restricted to his small office. Fossils, artifacts and rocks—humble tributes to his passions—arrayed in glass enclosed cases. Books lined the walls like a legion of hours.

The place was a sad, constricted mimicry of the palace of his mind, a bunker of wishes and wounds, where he had made do, hunkered down against loneliness and the inevitable dissolution of an unremarkable existence. Its inadequacy as a sanctuary had been made plain in one night by mysteries and wonders beyond comprehension— more than anything by Lark.

He had never known it was possible to need someone so desperately. He scowled, rubbing his arms, was seized by a babbling fit, groaned and cried out in anguish. He wanted to rip off his skin. The sudden change in Lark's attitude tormented him. He would not, could not accept it.

He was deposited mercilessly in the basement of his soul, where he had hidden away in crates and shadows all the parts of himself that he had neglected or disowned. Sealed them up in decisions to lead a safe and practical life, truncate his dreams, embrace ephemeral interests, squander his gifts on trivialities, and inure himself to the dissipation of his character.

He saw what he had become, and what he could have been, had meant to be, had imagined in youth that he would be. Strong and noble, decisive, quick, more than anything a man a woman could depend on. Not any woman, a woman for whom he yearned. A woman who could stand beside him with the same objective clarity of passion he felt for her, with whom he could bond in her soul, and she in his, that together they might defy the ravages of time with an ardor that would shame death.

The storm in his mind overwhelmed him, and he passed out on the floor of his living room. He lay there, a twisted figure, washed up on the shoals of his life, and all the humble treasures he had acquired, the bones and shards and fossils and books with which he had built the walls of his solitary domain, kept silent watch on his sleep.

He woke late, feeling wretched and disoriented, sat up and looked around with embarrassment at his belongings. He loved them too, and he had betrayed them; in his emotional crisis he had sullied the value they'd held for him, the support they had given. They were true and loyal companions, who had partnered his lonely days with small pleasures. It was unfair to disparage them.

He called his supervisor at the La Brea lab and told her he would not make it to work that day. He knew it would be many days before he returned to his job, if he ever did, but he was not prepared to tell her that.

Lark might be anywhere; he had no idea how to look for her. It occurred to him that he could start by retracing their steps. He cursed himself. He had wasted hours on dismay that he might have spent in motion. He scanned airline flights on his cell phone and booked a reservation on the next flight he could make to New York. Then he called an old friend who lived in Chelsea.

Sandy had met Gordon a decade ago, when he'd been hired by Sotheby's to authenticate a collection of fossils. They'd developed a close friendship, fueled by mutual interests, and deepened by philosophical accord. When Sandy moved to Los Angeles they'd fallen out of touch. He hadn't spoken to Gordon in over a year, and wasn't sure how he would be received. Gordon answered on the first ring, sounding surprised and pleased.

Sandy knew from experience that he was better off being direct with Gordon. "This isn't a casual call, Gordon; I need help. Something happened. I can't explain over the phone. I'm flying to New York this afternoon. Can we meet?"

The phone was silent a moment. When Gordon responded there was more warmth than uncertainty in his voice, and Sandy knew he'd taken the right tack. "Of course, Alexander. Let me know when your flight arrives, and I'll pick you up."

The mere hope of having an ally relieved a measure of his isolation.

He threw a bag together. On the verge of leaving he stopped at the threshold, unsure that he would return. He looked back at his beloved possessions, all the trinkets and books that had seemed valueless the night before. He thought of Lark and knew that he would go on, even at the expense of all he possessed. He wanted some memento to retain his connection with his past. He set down his suitcase and drifted hesitantly back into the living room, scanning the objects that he had acquired in digs and caves around the world. Each thing sparked a memory that made it keenly precious—fossils and pottery shards and tools. He started to reach for a fossilized trilobite, but his eyes fell on an old coin his grandfather had found in a field in France, during the war, and he pocketed that instead. Without another backwards glance, he left behind the life he had lived.

Waiting for his flight at LAX, he reviewed the events of the night before. He wondered if he had gone mad and imagined it all, it seemed so impossible. But every time Lark's face came to mind, the powerful feelings of love and yearning that spilled through him made everything else believable.

And every time he thought of the man in the dark, embroidered coat, a determination rose in him that would not be put down. He knew the man had worked some evil and abducted Lark. She had not gone with him willingly.

Gordon met him at LaGuardia. Sandy seized him in a tight embrace, then stepped back, embarrassed. He met no consternation in his old friend's eyes, only concern mixed with curiosity.

Gordon was heavier than Sandy remembered, his hair streaked with grey. But the person he was remained intact, the warmth and cheer that defined his character in full force in the cant of his presence.

Sandy wasn't in the mood to talk in the car, and Gordon left him alone with his thoughts. He drove them to his small Chelsea apartment, and Sandy saw immediately that his friend's circumstances echoed his own. Gordon, too, lived alone, surrounded by books and the small paintings and *objets d'art* he had collected over the years.

"Still with Sotheby's?"

"Oh, they'll never get rid of me. No one knows antique silver better than Gordon Cumberland."

Sandy had not expected to stay with Gordon, but Gordon installed him in his guest room without asking. Gordon fixed coffee for them and they sat in his living room. Sandy felt the tension ease from his shoulders.

"I'm sorry I haven't stayed in touch better," Sandy said.

"Oh, dear boy, life moves on. Don't trouble yourself."

"Are you seeing anyone?"

Gordon nodded wistfully. "He's too young for me." He shrugged. "Sometimes he stays the night. I am resigned to it. Horace keeps me company." At the sound of his name a dachshund curled in the corner raised its head and flapped its tail. "He's getting old. When he dies, I think I shall move back to England. Someplace in the country. I have the picture in my mind. I shall become a fixture, known for wandering the bowered lanes and quoting Browning to myself. But enough of me. You were distressed when you called. Tell your old friend everything."

"I'm afraid you'll think I've gone insane."

Gordon took a moment to respond. "Well," he said, "we're all a little cuckoo." He smiled reassuringly. "I'll give you a fair hearing and do my best to keep my skepticism in check."

Sandy couldn't think of any way to render his story plausible. He told Gordon everything as he remembered it. When he was done Gordon frowned and looked away, deep in thought. Sandy was afraid to hear his response. "I'm crazy, right? I've had a psychotic break."

Gordon shook his head. "The first thing we need to do is disabuse you of that notion. I know someone who might be able to help. Describe carefully where you found yourself when you arrived here last night."

Sandy stared at Gordon. "You believe me?"

"I do, Alexander. I'll explain why later. If my friend is going to help us, I need to call him right away, before he goes off duty."

"I don't ..." Sandy sighed. "I don't know what to say."

"Start by answering my question."

Sandy described everything he could remember seeing when Lark and he exited the mall. He'd been in such a daze he hadn't looked at street signs.

"That sounds like Union Square. Tell me, did you notice a bookstore behind you when you came out?"

Sandy shook his head. "I didn't look back."

Gordon grunted. "That's telling. I want you to relax now, Alexander. Rest and be comfortable, and leave this to me."

"Who are you going to call?" Sandy worried that Gordon would phone a psychiatrist or a hospital, or maybe even the police.

"There are cameras all around Union Square. I'm going to talk to someone who has access to the recordings."

Sandy's eyes widened with hope. "See if I'm there."

Gordon patted Sandy's knee. "Show you that you were—precisely."

Gordon went into his office and Sandy drifted around the apartment, eyeing Gordon's art collection. Watercolors of castles, cottages and gardens, etchings of people of bygone eras, in clothing of a century and more past. He lingered with a drawing of a backlit quill pen on a Victorian secretary desk that faced a window, an unreadable letter unfinished on the desktop.

Sandy went to Gordon's office and rapped softly on the door frame.

Gordon held his hand up, speaking on his cell phone. "Yes, around 9:30 last night … Thank you, Arthur, we'll be right over." He hung up and looked inquiringly at Sandy.

"I've remembered a few building features. I think you might be right about Union Square. In Chinatown there was a bank we passed that had Corinthian columns."

"Oh yes, I know that place."

"It was near the subway stop we exited. What did you find out?"

"My friend will help us."

They hailed a cab and took it to a police station on Thirty-fourth, between Seventh and Eighth. Along the way Sandy asked Gordon why he believed him.

"I'm not ready to tell you. When I do you'll understand. I will say that, in my work, I have known a great many prevaricators, and you are the farthest thing from a liar. You don't have it in you to concoct such a tale."

"That doesn't make me sane. It doesn't mean I didn't imagine it."

"The fact that you find your own story dubious lends it credence. But my reasons go beyond that. Let's see what we find at the police station, and then I'll explain." They were nearing the station, and Gordon nudged Sandy. "I told my friend you've lost your briefcase, which contained documents of earth-shattering importance. It could cost you your livelihood if you can't find it. You have no idea where you lost it, and we want to confirm that you still had it while you were in Union Square."

Gordon's friend met them in the lobby of the police station and led them through a security door. He was a heavyset young man with a taciturn attitude. As they made their way through the maze of offices, he spoke softly to Gordon and Sandy. "Not strictly kosher, letting you back here. Anyone asks, you're helping an attorney with a court case and can't talk about it."

"Thank you, Arthur," Gordon said. "I very much appreciate this."

"My grandmother's furniture got my kid in a private school. You did that, Mr. Cumberland. You don't have to thank me for anything."

Arthur led them to a room lined with banks of monitors. They scanned videos from several cameras covering the time period in question. It was odd watching people go by, unaware that their movements were recorded.

Gordon spotted him first. "There. Arthur, could you back that up, please?"

Sandy stared at the screen. At the sight of Lark leading him by hand down the sidewalk, he could barely keep himself from crying out.

"Is that her?" Gordon asked softly.

Sandy swallowed and nodded.

"I can see why you were so taken. She's magnificent."

Sandy watched himself be led off screen.

Arthur backed the recording up again. "I don't see a briefcase," he said, then squinted. "What the …" He backed the recording up yet again. Arthur froze it when Lark's image flickered, revealing an instant when she was missing from the video, leaving Sandy holding empty air. "That's not possible."

Sandy noticed someone else in the revolving door of the bookstore. "Let it run forward."

Arthur glanced back at him, frowning. He let the video run.

"There! Freeze it there."

The other person had come out of the store, and turned the same way down the sidewalk that Sandy and Lark had gone.

Sandy narrowed his gaze at the screen.

"Garritch."

Chapter Three

Back on the street, Sandy and Gordon got tired of trying to hail a cab, and Gordon didn't trust Uber, so they took the subway. They rode in silence to the stop nearest Gordon's flat.

Walking up the street by a small park grown with old oaks, Gordon said, "That was him, wasn't it—the man who took her?"

"Oh yeah, that was him." Sandy watched a group of kids play basketball in the park. "I'll never forget what you did for me today, Gordon. A better friend no man could ask for."

"Tell that to Ernst." Gordon sighed.

"When I get the chance, I will."

The night air was still and cool. In different circumstances Sandy would have enjoyed strolling with his friend in New York. He was too bundled with anxieties.

"If he pursued you here, it follows that he was pursuing her in Santa Monica."

Sandy hunched his shoulders. "What happened to me, Gordon? How is any of this possible? Who *is* he? Who is *she?*"

Gordon looked off awhile before answering. "I'm going to tell you a story, Sandy. Something I've never told anyone. Not a soul.

"When I was young, I used to have the most vivid dreams imaginable. I suppose you might call it a kind of lucid dreaming. But my lucid dreams didn't take place anywhere I was or had ever been, or indeed anywhere that exists on Earth, to my knowledge. I had my own dream world. I never talked about it, not even before the thing I'm about to tell you happened. I was sure very few people, if any, dreamed the way that I did, and I didn't want to be thought strange. Probably a symptom of a greater repression. Sexual attitudes weren't as relaxed back then. They're not all that relaxed, now. I hid a lot of things, even from myself. I dated women and tried to convince myself I was straight.

"Anyway, my dream world. I'd started dreaming that way when I was very young. I went places in my dreams that I don't know how to describe, other than to say they were fantastic and other worldly. Over time I sort of mapped them out—where they were, or where I imagined them to be, in relation to each other. I even developed the ability to determine, before I went to sleep, where I would go.

"I knew people in my dream world. I had friends—people with whom I was familiar. There was this beautiful black waiter in a bar, with the face of Adonis—"

"Gordon!" Sandy stopped and stared at his friend.

"I know, dear boy, I know; let me finish."

They continued walking. "The thing I couldn't remember upon waking was conversations. I remembered having long interactions with the people but nothing of the substance of what we said to each other. Then, one night, that changed.

"I was in Munich. This was thirty years ago. I hadn't been with Sotheby's long; I was still in my apprenticeship. We were appraising an estate for the heirs of some deceased dowager.

"Anyway, one night I dreamed of visiting this bar—very like the one you described, yes—and there was some altercation. I can't remember what it was about—I wasn't involved in it—but some people were forced to leave. That waiter brought me a free cocktail as an apology for the disturbance. I was thoroughly smitten with the fellow, and we had a kind of moment, if you know what I mean. A bit later he came back and sat with me.

"That one time, I remember what we said to each other quite clearly. I have no context to explain any of it, but it has stayed with me, nevertheless.

"I asked if the bar were going to have to move, by which I meant relocate, physically, to another place. It was not, in my dream, situated in New York, but in some other city that, as I said, I'm not sure exists. It was a basement establishment, and in all other aspects much as the place you describe, but I had no sense of it having an actual location in the world.

"The waiter responded that he hoped not—hoped it wouldn't be forced to move—because the bill to Time would be very steep. He said 'Time' with an understood capital, as if personified, like Chronos in the old myths. And I understood him—it was a very matter-of-fact exchange.

"Just then there was a kind of explosion. The door burst open, and a great rabble poured into the bar. The waiter fixed on them with the most ferocious expression— all business, suddenly. He made a strange gesture at me, and immediately I woke up.

"Except, you see, I didn't wake up where I'd gone to sleep."

Sandy stopped again. A tall man in a white hat and a short man in a leather jacket walked by. Children screeched in a playground.

"Yes," Gordon said, "you understand now why I had so little difficulty believing your tale."

"What happened?"

"Well, I was terrified, as you can imagine. I'd gone to sleep in my room at the Torbräu in Munich, and awakened in the Saint James in Paris. Not only that but my clothes and belongings had come with me. Suits in the closet, shirts and undergarments neatly arranged in the dresser, toiletries organized according to my habits in the bathroom.

"It was the wee hours when I awoke. By morning I'd collected myself enough to call my boss in Munich. Told him some nonsense I'd concocted to explain my sudden absence and said I'd be back the following day. I spent the rest of the day wandering Paris, trying to sort myself out.

"It was several nights before I managed to go back to sleep. Sheer exhaustion. But I've never returned to my dream world since." He sighed.

They stopped in front of Gordon's apartment building and Gordon lit a cigarette. Sandy had quit smoking but he took one when Gordon offered.

"I don't know what happened to you, Sandy. But I know absolutely that the reality we perceive is not the only one. There is another, right here beside us, and it doesn't operate as ours does. It doesn't obey the physical laws with which we are familiar. And in that other reality, terrible forces hold sway. Those forces have brushed up against you, my son."

They went in and rode the elevator most of the way up in silence.

"What are you going to do?" Gordon asked.

"Look for that bar, for starters."

"I'd like to accompany you on your search."

"I'd welcome your company, Gordon. But I don't want to put you at risk."

"I can look after myself. And *I* would welcome the opportunity to answer a few questions of my own."

Chapter Four

That night Sandy couldn't sleep. He kept thinking about Lark, praying she was all right. He was spared imagining her in horrible situations, because he could not imagine what those situations might be. He could only see her suffering or dead from her wound, and that was horrible enough. Her abductor had seemed, in the instant before he took her, concerned for her, and Sandy took what comfort he could from that impression.

It was an impossible coincidence that he would form a chance friendship with someone who had had an experience similar to his, or to one he would have later in their acquaintanceship. And Gordon was the first person to whom Sandy had thought to reach out. No, there was more than coincidence at work there.

Sandy heard movement in the living room. He thought it must be Gordon, but, as he listened, came alert. It didn't sound like Gordon. Sandy sat up.

Someone else was in the apartment.

He climbed out of bed as silently as he could, crept across the corridor to the threshold of the living room.

City light from the street outlined the curtains and dimly illumined furniture and the pictures on the walls. Sandy saw no movement, stepped cautiously into the room.

"Gordon?"

Someone jumped on him and bore him to the ground, pinning his arms with their legs. Sandy struggled to get free. He felt a sharp point against his throat.

"Be still," a gruff voice said, "or I'll cut you."

Sandy stopped struggling.

"Where is it?" the voice asked.

"What?"

"Don't muck me about, laddie. You took it or she gave it you."

"I don't know what you're talking about. Get off of me!"

The lights came on. The person who held him was a bearded brute with black eyes and a knurled forehead. The man looked back at Gordon, who held a pistol trained on him.

The man's eyes widened. *"You!"* He jumped off Sandy and was out of the apartment in a flash, knocking a lamp off an end table en route. Sandy leapt up and went after him, but there was no one in the outer hall when he got there. Gordon came up behind him. They listened, searched the hall end to end, opened the door to the stairwell and listened. Sandy's attacker seemed to have vanished.

They went back to Gordon's apartment. Sandy righted the fallen lamp and end table.

"Neither one of us is going to sleep tonight," Gordon said. "We might as well put insomnia to use. What do you say we look for that red door?"

Sandy took a quick shower and dressed. Gordon had fixed coffee by the time he returned to the kitchen. Gordon poured him a cup and they sat at the table in the breakfast nook.

"Did you recognize him? Someone from that club, maybe?" Sandy asked.

Gordon shrugged. "Maybe. Vaguely."

"He recognized you."

"Yes, I got that. But I'm asking myself to remember someone from a dream I had thirty years ago."

"But that would be where you know him from—your dream world. You're sure."

"Sure? No. It seems an obvious association to make."

Sandy looked down at the table. "He was looking for something."

"What?"

"I don't know. But he thought I had it."

They watched each other in silence. Gordon worked his lips. "Dear boy, I can't help thinking your young woman set you up somehow."

The same thought had occurred to Sandy but he'd rejected it. "I'm not going to sour my memories of her with mistrust, Gordon. Not yet."

Gordon was embarrassed. "Apologies, Alexander. I'll go chew some hard soap."

Sandy reached across the table and grasped his friend's hand. "Never apologize to me for anything."

They set out just after one a.m. and took a subway train into Chinatown. They found the bank fronted by Corinthian columns. From that point Sandy's memory gave them less to go on. They searched for two hours before Sandy spotted a furniture store that seemed familiar. They crossed the street for a closer look. Beside the store they found stairs leading down to a red door.

"Did you bring your gun?" Sandy asked.

Gordon patted the left breast of his jacket.

They descended the steps cautiously. A small, flat panel had been nailed to the door, covering the place where a slot might have been. Sandy tried the knob; the door was open. No subterranean nightclub lay within but an underground kitchen bustling with Asians preparing bulk quantities of foods. The workers were so engaged in their labors that they hardly spared Sandy and Gordon a glance.

"It would seem our supernatural bar has moved on again," Gordon said.

They kept searching anyway, on the slim chance there might be another stairwell somewhere with an identical red door at its bottom.

"It's going to be morning soon," Gordon said at last. "I'm hungry. We've been at this for hours."

They took a subway downtown. Gordon led Sandy to a delicatessen he liked that opened early.

"The lox and onion scramble is excellent," Gordon said, as they took a table.

New York never slept. Five a.m. and the place was bustling. Sandy let Gordon order for him. When the food came he ate a few bites and pushed the plate away.

"How am I going to find her, Gordon? It's hopeless."

"I never permit myself to think that about anything, my friend."

"Can you remember anything from your dream experiences that might help? I feel like an idiot asking."

"I'd say we've strayed sufficiently from the norm to dispense with embarrassment." Gordon smiled. "I never related my dream world to waking reality. Other than the bar, there weren't many corollaries. The cities were so fantastic, I'm sure they don't exist. Not in this world. There were a lot of caves …"

"Go on."

"It's so long ago, it's grown very vague. It's strange to think of, let alone talk about it. I'd rather pushed it all from my mind."

"What did you do, in those dreams?"

"Just wandered, mostly. Had a lot of conversations with very strange folk that, as I said, I've never been able to recall. Some of the people I met weren't human. Preternaturally beautiful winged creatures, more like fairies than angels. Oh, it all seems so fanciful. Can it really have been real?"

"Some of it was."

"Yes, there's no doubt of that. I can't stop wondering if there's some purpose behind it, us being drawn together." He turned his head in thought. "You know, I think I've remembered how it began for me."

"The dreaming?"

"Yes, the first time I dreamed in that way. It parallels your experience with your young woman. I was in a European village, on a cobbled way between old row buildings and a church, and there was this young boy. This was long before I'd come to terms with my sexuality, but I thought he was beautiful. Very cheerful and high-spirited. He just walked straight up to me and said something that made me laugh. I think in that moment something changed in me, something very profound. It was like you said with your young woman—suddenly all I wanted was to be with him.

"He took my hand, and led me along to a narrow alley, at the end of which was a great wooden door."

"Was it painted red?"

"You know, I think it might have been. Yes, I'm sure of it. And there was a slot in it, too. The boy knocked and said something to the person who looked out. The door opened and we passed into a completely different place, on a hillside overlooking a city of crystal spires and impossible trees. My God, I haven't thought of that in forever."

Sandy looked out the window. Morning traffic was on the move, the sidewalks already filling with pedestrians. He noticed someone watching them from across the street, slapped his hands flat on the table and stood up. "Gordon."

Gordon looked where Sandy did. "Is that him, the one who attacked you?"

"You're fucking right it is."

They both lurched out of the booth and ran out of the diner, the waiter calling after them. The man across the street saw them and bolted. Gordon and Sandy dodged through traffic and chased him. He turned down a side street.

Half a block on Sandy noticed that Gordon wasn't with him. He was a hundred feet back, heaving for breath. He waved Sandy on.

Sandy chased the man down stairs into the underground maze of pedestrian tunnels. The man reached a barrier of turnstiles and jumped over them, agile as a cat.

Sandy pushed through the crowd, jumping up to see over heads. He wasn't as graceful getting over the turn-stiles. A cop shouted at him.

He pursued the man down another long tunnel and a flight of stairs to a platform. The man slammed his way through commuters waiting for trains. When he got to the far end of the platform he jumped down into the rail bed.

Sandy cursed and jumped down after him. No trains in the tunnel right then, but they would be coming. The tunnel was dark. His quarry grew dim in the distance.

Sandy ran into the darkness, mindful of the location of the rails. He dropped into a loping gait, letting his fingers brush the wall on his right.

Something changed. The wall dropped away and Sandy stopped. He swung his arms out and couldn't feel anything. A heaviness settled into the air, with a dank, mineral wetness. He looked back but the darkness had become absolute. He couldn't see anything in any direction. Adrenaline receded and his skin crawled with goose-bumps. An inchoate sense settled upon him that he was not where he had been.

Faintly, and then more clearly, his eyes adjusted to light of a different character, and his surroundings became visible. He was no longer in the subway tunnel but a cave, a vast cavern spanned vertically, at regular intervals, by immense mineral columns. The cavern was like a great hall constructed by slow, natural processes.

Someone seized him from behind and he felt a knife at his throat.

"You don't belong here, laddie."

Sandy recognized the voice of the man who had attacked him in Gordon's apartment. He felt the man's breath on his neck.

Sandy swallowed. "I want to know what's going on."

"Shh! Quiet now. It's not given you to know."

A tear leaked from Sandy's eye. "I just want to find Lark. She's in trouble."

The man didn't respond. They stayed fixed like that for a moment. The man loosened his grip and the knife withdrew from Sandy's throat. When he let go Sandy spun around.

"Easy," the man said. He wasn't a large person, shorter than Sandy, but there was a palpable capacity for violence about him.

"Why did you break into Gordon's apartment? What were you looking for?"

The man grinned sourly. "You're so feckin' lost. You're a blind man what's stumbled into an elephant."

"Help me, then. I can tell you know what I'm talking about. Give me something to go on."

The man grimaced but didn't respond.

"Your accent—you sound Scottish. Should I go there? Should I go to England?"

The man stepped forward warningly. "I'm Quick, laddie. I'm from everywhere."

Sandy held his hands out, placatingly. "Just tell me something—anything. *Help* me."

"You think you can save her? Set up house in some cozy with the birdies singin'?"

"She told me that she loves me."

The man rolled his eyes and sneered. "You don't know who she is. Or what. She's a font of pure fire, laddie. You get too close, she'll burn you to a cinder." He looked Sandy up and down. "Knight-errant." He growled in disgust. "Not hardly." With a snap he thrust his knife forward and touched the point to Sandy's forehead. "Sleep," he said.

Consciousness left Alexander like sand spilling from a fractured hourglass.

Chapter Five

An oncoming train startled Sandy awake. He leapt to his feet, his heart racing. He was in a maintenance alcove off a subway tunnel. He flattened against the door until the train passed and stayed there, gasping for breath.

He rubbed his face and tried to orient himself. He didn't want to venture down any more railway tunnels. He tried the door and found it open. Inside, a long flight of stairs led up.

The stairs led to a maintenance corridor. Sandy flipped a mental coin and went right, eventually coming to a door that opened onto a subway platform where a few people waited. A couple of them frowned at him. Sandy patted his pockets, pulled out his cell phone and checked the time. 8:32 p.m. He'd been unconscious the length of the day.

He made his way up to the street, found himself a few blocks from Times Square. He walked to Broadway and hailed a cab, gave the driver Gordon's address.

He could see nothing the same as he had. The dark world he rode through, people in search of love, money, whatever their quests—they were dreamers unaware that they were asleep.

The cabbie dropped him in front of Gordon's apartment building. The doorman, a lean, elderly man given to bygone formality, let him in.

"Mr. Cumberland has some workmen up there."

"Oh. Okay, thanks."

"Could you please tell him that a neighbor has complained about the noise? I called but he didn't answer."

"Sure."

The doorman followed Sandy to the elevator. "Remind him, if you don't mind, that he's supposed to give us thirty days notice before having work done, so we can notify the other residents."

"All right."

"And work should stop by seven." The doorman tapped his watch.

"I'll tell him."

Sandy rode the elevator to the seventh floor, wondering what he would do next. He hoped Gordon would have some ideas. Sandy had never felt so grateful for a friend.

He rang the doorbell but Gordon didn't answer. Sandy noticed the door was ajar. He pushed it open cautiously.

"Gordon?"

No answer.

The interior of the apartment was dark. Sandy flipped on the lights. The place was a shambles, furniture overturned, Gordon's small decorative treasures strewn on the floor, smashed and broken, paintings askew, some slashed, some thrown down. More than a search had happened here; the level of destruction spoke of wanton vandalism, rage, hatred …

Sandy stepped through the wreckage. "Gordon?"

"Here!" a pained voice cried.

Sandy hurried to Gordon's bedroom. The lights didn't work, but light filtering in from the living room revealed a similar state of affairs: furniture awry, the mattress ripped open, drawers turned out, clothes from the closet flung down in a heap.

Sandy heard movement on the far side of the bed. Gordon was sprawled on the floor by the window, reaching for him. Sandy knelt by his friend, took his hand.

"Sandy …"

"I'm here, Gordon. What happened?" Sandy felt wetness on his hand. In city light from the window he saw black stains on the carpet and Gordon's abdomen. Gordon's shirt was soaked in blood.

"I'll call an ambulance." Sandy, shaking, fumbled with his cell phone.

"No." Gordon clutched Sandy's collar and pulled him close. "Listen—listen to me." His voice was raspy, his breathing labored.

Sandy couldn't get the damn phone to cooperate with blood on his fingers and Gordon pulling at him.

Gordon held him insistently. "*Listen!* I remember. I remember everything. In Paris—when I woke up in Paris—there was a coin in my jacket. The safe behind my desk. You'll know it. Not like any coin you've seen. Twelve—Twenty-Four—Seventeen."

"Okay, Gordon. Let me call ..."

Gordon gripped him tighter. "You're in awful danger, Alexander. I'm sorry. But listen to me, you're right about the girl. Do you understand? You're *right* about her."

Sandy couldn't see where Gordon had been stabbed. "I'm going to take care of you ..."

"Tell Ernst I love him." Gordon released his grasp. "Poor Horace tried to protect me." In the pale city light, the grimace on his face became a grin. "Bastards didn't get shit." Life left his eyes.

"Gordon?" Sandy clutched him. "Stay with me." He felt for a pulse, but knew it was over. "Oh, Gordon." Sandy held his dead friend's hand and bowed his head.

He gently closed Gordon's eyes, then found himself in the bathroom, washing his hands, not knowing how he'd gotten there. He stared at himself in the mirror. His collar was bloodstained where Gordon had grabbed him. He went to his bedroom. His luggage had been rifled through. He took off the bloodstained shirt and put on a clean one, remembered what Gordon had told him.

The Victorian water color that had concealed Gordon's safe had been torn from the wall and thrown on the floor, its frame cracked and the glass shattered. The edges of the safe had been pried at. Sandy turned the dial, entering the combination. He reduced the number numerologically as he did so, remembering Gordon's eccentricities. Twelve, twenty-four, seventeen: the resulting sum was eight, the number often mis-associated with wealth and power—its underlying character was balance. Gordon's favorite number—turned on its side it became an infinity symbol.

Inside the safe were stacks of papers: titles, bearer bonds and a will, the latter naming Ernst as Gordon's beneficiary. Sandy placed the papers on the desk. At the back of the safe was a small, blue jeweler's box that opened clamshell style. Inside was a coin about the size of a silver dollar that looked to be made of brass. Its edge was not round but twelve-sided. On one face was the image of a blind-folded woman beneath two crossed swords, on the other an eye encircled by a laurel wreath.

Gordon was wrong; Sandy had seen such a coin before. He fished the one his grandfather had given him out of his wallet and compared it with Gordon's. They were identical.

CHAPTER SIX

Sandy started to call the police and stopped himself. He was not living in the same world he had little more than a day ago. Every action he took now had to be gauged against the designs of unseen movers. All he had to go on was wits and instinct. The police couldn't help him and might get in his way.

He pulled on his jacket, hunted around and found Gordon's keys and cell phone, pocketed them. He spotted the barrel of Gordon's handgun sticking out from beneath a mess of papers, picked it up and held it uncertainly. He thought of Gordon, dead in his own bedroom, made sure the safety was on and stuck the handgun in the back of his pants. He checked in the bathroom mirror to make sure his jacket covered it.

He returned to Gordon's bedroom and stood a moment looking at his friend. He noticed the dachshund's small body, lifeless by the corner of the bed. The killings were so evil and pointless; he wanted the bastards who had done it. It came to him that they must have left shortly before he arrived. He bolted out of the apartment and took the elevator to the lobby, composing himself on the way down.

Sandy approached the doorman, doing his best to be nonchalant.

"The men working in Mr. Cumberland's apartment—he asked me to try to catch them." Sandy heard the quaver in his voice but the doorman didn't seem to notice. "They left some tools behind. He mislaid his cell phone and doesn't have their number written down."

The doorman nodded. "Happens all the time. That's why I still keep a handwritten address book. But they haven't come through here. They might have left out of the garage."

Sandy ran for the stairwell.

"Did you happen to convey my message?" the doorman called after him.

Sandy stopped in the doorway. "They finished their work."

He took the stairs two at a time down to the garage, opened the door at the bottom a crack and peeked out. He heard voices—two men arguing. Quietly, he stepped through the doorway.

"… get into that safe. We have to go back."

"We have to get out of here. Whoever pounded on the wall has called somebody. I tell you to be quiet and you go nuts, tearing the place up."

"We don't have time for niceties."

"You didn't have to kill him. There are going to be repercussions—"

"He shouldn't have resisted. We need that coin. You want to tell Garritch we let that bullshit knight-errant get hold of it? Maybe you don't mind being stuck in that hell-hole the rest of your life but I do."

Sandy crept through the garage, keeping to the shadows. He peeked around a square pillar and saw the men. The tall one wore a white hat and a long, tan raincoat. The short man was built like a fighter. Sandy had seen them somewhere before. It came to him: they'd walked by Gordon and him last night on the street.

Rage got the better of stealth. Sandy stepped from behind the pillar and marched toward them, pulling Gordon's gun.

The men saw him and bolted.

"Hey!" Sandy shouted. He ran after them, pointed the gun at the ceiling and squeezed the trigger. Nothing happened. He cursed, flicked off the safety, pulled the trigger again. He flinched at the loudness of the report. The arguers froze at the exit door.

"Fucking hold it right there." Sandy pointed the gun at them.

They stared at Sandy a beat. The short man said, "Screw this," flung the door open and ran out. The tall man followed.

"Hey!" Sandy tucked the gun back in his pants and ran after them, cursing his own stupidity.

Traffic was grid-locked on the street. The two men dodged between cars and split up on the other side. The tall man was the slower runner so Sandy went right, after him, to the end of the block and left around the corner. There were more pedestrians on the broader thoroughfare; both Sandy and his quarry earned shouts and curses, busting through them. They caught the attention of an overweight cop coming out of a deli. "That son-of-a-bitch is a murderer!" Sandy shouted, running by. He glanced back. The cop was talking on his radio but not joining pursuit.

The tall man increased the distance between them. Sandy pushed himself but he was out of shape, breathing hard. The tall man slammed through people exiting stairs to the subway. Someone called Sandy a motherfucker as he forced his way down.

At the bottom Sandy met a maze—a broad junction of tunnels, people going every which way. He searched for the white hat, spotted it, ran through a Reggae group playing "I Shot the Sheriff," interrupting their song and sending their tips bowl flying. The tall man went through a turnstile. Sandy snatched a ticket from a woman coming the other way and let himself through, a stream of high-pitched vitriol trailing after him.

The white hat went down another broad flight of stairs. The platform at the bottom was crowded. Sandy spotted the hat and a balled tan raincoat on a bench, a young couple sitting near them staring after someone. Sandy tracked their gaze.

"Hey, man, you don't want your coat?" the young man called out.

"I'll take the hat," the woman said, trying it on.

A train arrived and people started boarding. He spotted a tall man with a thin face moving on board, caught him glancing nervously, sidelong, in Sandy's direction.

Sandy waited to the last second and pushed onboard the nearest car. The doors closed and he shouldered his way through passengers to the end of the car, crossed to the next one. He spotted the tall man and pushed toward him.

The tall man didn't move, gave up pretense and met Sandy's gaze with grim readiness. Sandy stopped pressing forward and returned the man's stare. The train switched tracks and the lights blacked out. When they came on again, the man was gone.

CHAPTER SEVEN

Sandy searched the crowded cars but couldn't find the tall man. He supposed he must have translocated, in some ethereal way, like Lark had; though he wondered, if he could do that, why he hadn't done it sooner.

Maybe the stars weren't aligned right, what did he know.

He got off at the next stop, watched passengers exit until the train pulled away, but didn't see the tall man. Then he spotted him still on board, waving through a window. Sandy shouted and slapped the side of the departing train.

The train receded down the tunnel. A great helplessness sank through Sandy. He'd lost his only lead and didn't know what to do.

He opened Gordon's cell phone and called Ernst. A snarling rap song assailed his ear, followed by a beep. "Ernst, Gordon Cumberland is dead. He was murdered in his apartment. Call the police when you get this message. Gordon wanted you to know that he loved you. He made you the sole beneficiary of his will." Sandy clicked off. He'd never met Ernst and felt no sympathy for him.

He took the subway back to Chinatown and wandered aimlessly down streets that had become familiar, drifted beyond the areas Gordon and he had combed. Hours passed. He happened upon an all-night diner and went in, ordered a pastrami sandwich. He was hungry, but when the food came he had no interest in it.

He noticed a rack of cigarettes by the cash register. He paid his bill and bought a lighter and a pack of the brand Gordon smoked. He asked the cashier where the restrooms were. She pointed down a long hall at the back of the diner.

About fifty feet in, the hall turned right, and twice that distance on, Sandy found the bathroom by a metal door with a bar latch under an exit sign at the hall's end. He went in and relieved himself. When he came out he didn't want to go back to the restaurant so he left through the back door.

He found himself in an abbreviated alley walled off at its near end. A tin-hatted fixture above the door illumined a circle of asphalt if front of it. Sandy opened the pack of cigarettes, drifted outside the circle, noticed three youths talking by a dumpster near the street. He fed a cigarette to his mouth and lit it, took a long drag and blew a stream of smoke at the stars.

Travel well, my friend.

"Hey, spare a loosey?"

The three youths came toward him.

"What?"

The one in the lead, a skinny Asian in a paisley shirt, mimed smoking a cigarette.

"Oh." Sandy nodded, his guard going up. "Sure." He shook a couple of cigarettes forward and held out the pack. The other two boys were bigger, one heavily muscled.

"Hey, give us whole pack!" The skinny boy snatched the pack away and handed it to his friends. "Very generous! Thank you so much!" He laughed and flipped open a butterfly knife. "Now money, boy-boy!"

Sandy reached back for his gun but it wasn't there. He'd lost it somewhere without noticing.

"Give up your wallet, mister," the muscular kid said. He was like a machine, dead in the eyes.

Sandy was damned if he would. The coins were in his wallet. They were his only link to Lark. The memory of her starburst eyes flashed through his mind and his will turned to stone. He backed toward the wall at the inner end of the alley.

"Hey, don't run away!" The skinny boy laughed. "We friendly!" His friends spread out, blocking Sandy's way out of the alley.

The atmosphere seemed to thicken, and an elusive noise, like crackling parchment and grinding steel, etched the air. Another figure stood at the open end of the alley, backlit in silhouette by streetlight. The person wore some kind of elongated hat and a long coat with a heavy mantle about the shoulders.

The person advanced into the alley with a slow, deliberate gait and a disquieting aspect of purpose.

The youths made way, the muscular one jumping back. "The fuck!?"

The person came near enough for the illumination of the tin-hatted fixture to clarify his appearance. A stranger creature Sandy had never beheld, not in life or in dream. *It*—Sandy could not be sure of the person's sex—had the head and face of an infant atop what appeared, from the height and size of its garments, to be the body of a grown adult. The head was wrapped in a white sock, like a nun's wimple, exposing only its face. Around that was a structure like a stiff hood, atop which rested a large skull with a long beak. The person wore a heavy cloak that reached the ground, concealing any impression of its body, the garment's shoulders festooned with a voluminous mantle of black feathers. A woven belt stitched in and out of the cloak at waist-level, fastened in front by a metal clasp bearing the emblems of Alpha and Omega. From the belt hung a leather chord to which were fastened three small primate skulls. The cloak had an elusive shimmer in the dim light, its velvety, purple and black fabric flashing implications of myriad symbols. In its left hand the person held a staff with a triumvirate cross at its apex.

The being fixed its infant gaze on Sandy. In those small eyes was a presence and power that knew no allegiance to age, and Sandy knew that the weird reality he sought had found him.

"Knight-errant," the being said, its androgynous voice wavering, as if emanating through liquid. "You seek entrance to the school."

The hoodlums regained their bravado and closed in around the strange person. It did not respond to them, nor show any sign of unease.

"Cray-cray got mad threads, check it out."

"Hey, Cosplay, you take us party. We so sad, nothing to do."

The boy with the knife grabbed the being's shoulder. His eyes went wide and his mouth gaped open. Veins in his arms and neck became visibly distended and his eyes rolled back. The color drained from his face.

"K.J., you all right?"

The skinny boy's skin blackened. Fiery cracks formed in it, as if he burned from within. His companions caught him as he fell. He collapsed into ash in their arms.

The muscular boy's eyes weren't dead anymore, when he looked at Sandy. He and his surviving friend ran from the alley.

Sandy wanted to run too, but he didn't. He wanted answers.

He swallowed. "What are you?"

"I am Cabal the Ageless, Hierophant of the Labyrinth of Souls. All who seek entry to the school must apply to me."

"I don't know anything about a school. A woman I know was abducted, and I want to find her."

"Desire is irrelevant," Cabal said. "Your quest is at hand. There have been violations. You are Knight-errant, appointed by the Quints. You must pass through the Labyrinth, peel from the personality by which you know yourself all shadows, and understand your nature. You must become unmasked to yourself."

"I'll do whatever is necessary to find Lark, and deal with the son-of-a-bitch who kidnapped her." Sandy wondered if the Hierophant was blind. It stared in his direction without really looking at him. The being seemed to know its surroundings by another faculty than sight.

An idiot grin grew on its infant lips. "You must demonstrate to me some expertise, show that you have studied an art with diligence."

Sandy thought a moment. He pointed at the skull mounted on the Hierophant's hood. "That's a pterodactyl skull. Fledgling, from its size." He pointed at the skulls hanging from the Hierophant's belt. "The top one is oldest, Neanderthal, at a guess. The one below it is high Asian, Mongolian possibly, by the cheekbones and orbits. The bottom one is Caucasoid, possibly French ancestry. They're all the skulls of pre-pubescent children."

The Hierophant's grin broadened. "That is sufficient." It extended its hand. "The coin."

Sandy stared at the hand—a man's hand, heavily calloused, the hand of a laborer. He did not know what species of creature it was that stood before him, that accessorized with skulls and wore a cloak that killed. This was the third time in two days someone had tried to take a coin from him, and he did not feel disposed to relinquish one without explanation or assurance.

"What coin?" he said.

The Hierophant's vacuous gaze did not waver, nor its expression alter.

Sandy tried another tack. "You say it is within your power to grant me entrance to a school. What kind of school? You say what I want is irrelevant. I do not accept that. I will not see the woman I love held against her will. This way that you offer, will it lead to her?"

"Of love I know only that it is a force of nature," the Hierophant said.

"That is not what I asked."

"If you seek to enter unto the mysteries of the Quick, there is no other way."

"Why did you come to me? Why should I trust you?"

The Hierophant did not answer. Its hand remained extended, providing nothing else to go on.

"May I not refuse?"

"Of course." The Hierophant withdrew its hand and turned to go.

Sandy hadn't expected that. If this creature spoke the truth, he might lose his last chance, here, to find Lark.

"Wait."

The Hierophant turned back and waited impassively. Sandy looked at the ashes of the boy who had touched the creature's cloak. Whatever the path offered here proved to be, no other he had known in his life up to now was any more sure to serve him.

"All right."

The Hierophant extended its hand again. It was a different hand, now, slender and feminine. Sandy took out his wallet and extracted the coin he had taken from Gordon's safe. He placed it in the Hierophant's hand.

"Witness," the Hierophant said, keeping its hand extended, palm up, with the coin resting in it. "Your father, William Creaze, was a lineman for the power company. He died when you were young, repairing a junction during an electrical storm. Your mother was an aspiring artist who succumbed to drink. You were raised by your grandfather on your father's side, Emanuel Creaze, whose wife died before you were born. He entered the European Theater through Omaha Beach in the conflict known as World War II. He was an entomologist. From him you acquired your interest in examining the ages of the world. You have had little contact with your extended family, and know even less of your ancestors, though you bear their footprints on the terrain of your being. In spite of your competency with your chosen profession, you have never felt at peace with your place in the world. You believe in love and kindness and the inherent worth of humanity. Those beliefs will be challenged in what lies before you."

While the Hierophant spoke the coin began to glow. It turned red, then white, and Sandy felt heat emanate from it. The coin lost cohesion, and sank into the Hierophant's hand. It vanished, then, leaving no trace upon the being's skin.

The Hierophant plucked a feather from the mantle of its cloak. "Extend your hand."

Sandy hesitated, glancing at the ashen remains of the hapless K. J.

"My cloak kills only when it is touched without my permission," the Hierophant said.

Sandy swallowed and extended his hand.

"Remain still," the Hierophant said, and placed the black feather in Sandy's palm. Like the coin, the feather became hot. When it began to burn him, he did not let himself flinch; he did not want to test the Hierophant's forgiveness. The feather turned red, as if, like the coin, it were made of metal. Pain passed the threshold of what Sandy thought he could bear, but he did bear it. The feather turned white hot; he thought it would burn through his hand. He stifled the reflex to cry out, and discovered that he possessed the capacity to view the information of his senses from a detached perspective, and regard them dispassionately as phenomena.

The feather lost cohesion and sank into his hand, leaving no trace upon his skin. But his transcendence of the pain was seared on his memory.

"You are the Knight-errant. You have stepped to the threshold of your quest. If you turn from it now, your life will be marked by vacuity and ignominious servitude. If you embrace it, you will pass through the veils of the unknown, and none may say what will become of you.

"You may now ask two questions, one insipid and one existential."

Sandy stared at his hand, worked his fingers. It felt normal, as if nothing had happened to it. At the same time he felt changes he couldn't have named taking place in his body and being.

He took a guess at what the Hierophant might consider an insipid question. "How do I find Lark?" he asked.

"The Quints of Love is held in the Citadel of the Maimed. Her memory has been occluded, and she believes her only purpose is pleasure. Her other aspects are cloaked from my sight, but Garritch seeks them. To find her you must penetrate Time and Distance, and cross the Endless Plain. You will lose all memory of yourself and require a talisman to reclaim your identity." The Hierophant's hand withdrew into the folds of its cloak, and reemerged, withered and old, bearing a vernier caliper that it held out to Sandy.

Sandy steeled himself against further pain and accepted the instrument. It remained cool to his touch. It was the very type of caliper he had been searching for when he met Lark. In his familiar life he would have used it to measure and catalogue small fossilized bone fragments. He turned it over in his hand and peered at it. In black ink on the handle were the letters "A C." He'd written them himself with an indelible marker.

It wasn't *like* the caliper he'd lost, it *was* the caliper he'd lost.

"You have one question remaining," the Hierophant said.

Sandy wanted to ask how the hell the Hierophant had gotten his caliper. He suspected that would be a waste of his question. Existential, he thought. The host of questions he had on that count crowded his mind irreducibly, from *'Is there a God?'* to *'Why am I alive?'* They were too sprawling, too formless, and he feared the answers the Hierophant might give. He needed something specific to his circumstances.

He remembered something the Hierophant had said at the start of their exchange. "You said there have been violations. What does that mean?"

"There are those who would render the future change-less, save in accordance to their whims. They will fail, but in their madness may cause much destruction.

"Your questions are expired. Return home and put your affairs in order. In two days time, return to the place where you met the Quints. Be there at the time of your first encounter with her. The way will open. Once you cross the threshold, there will be no turning back. You have gained entry through the Way of Discs. If you wish to return to this world, you will have to acquire another coin."

The Hierophant turned and stood over the ashes of the dead youth. It opened its mouth and inhaled, and the ashes were drawn up into its mouth in a swirling stream until not a particle remained.

"Farewell, Knight-errant. I wish you success."

The Hierophant walked off toward the entrance of the alley. In a few steps it vanished, like smoke eaten by a vagrant gust.

Chapter Eight

Sandy booked a flight back to Los Angeles out of Newark, and took a cab to the airport. He tried to be as inconspicuous as possible, not sure if the police would be looking for him. Hopefully, Ernst had received his message by now, and contacted the authorities. The part of Sandy that had always believed in his society, however beleaguered it became, that took for granted that the toilet would flush and the lights turn on and that people in public service by and large did their best, nagged at him that he should present himself for questioning and report what he knew that wouldn't sound crazy. But that part clung to a world he no longer inhabited. He had already left it behind. He knew the crimes committed in Gordon's apartment would never be cleared from the books.

He arrived in Los Angeles without incident, retrieved his car from the car park and drove to his apartment. On the way he stopped at the bank and took all but a thousand dollars out of his account. He didn't know if money would be of use where he was going, but it seemed best to prepare for contingencies.

All the while, anxieties about the course he was taking warred with his feelings for Lark. She was so distant she seemed like a dream fading inside of a dream. He feared that he would wake up and lose her before he could fix her image in his mind. But he remembered her kneeling beside him, on their bed among the stars, and the power and truth of that moment banished doubt and uncertainty. He would drown in a sea of forgetfulness before he would betray that moment, or relinquish his quest to honor that love.

What was anything worth without that?

He knew something was wrong before he opened the door. An inner sense he wasn't used to attending warned him. His apartment was in a worse state than Gordon's. The glass display cases were all shattered, their contents strewn about the floor, his books thrown down from the shelves. As in Gordon's apartment, the vandalism went beyond searching. The evidence of rage was everywhere.

A black man in a business jacket sat in an armchair, calmly regarding him. Sandy whirled and found his way blocked by two uniformed policemen.

"Mister Creaze, we'd like a word with you," the man in the business jacket said. He stood and flipped open his badge. "Detective James, LAPD."

Sandy sighed in exasperation. "I did *not* kill Gordon Cumberland."

"Yes, we know that. You made kind of a spectacle of yourself chasing the man who did. What we're curious about is why you didn't make a report to the authorities. The NYPD is particularly curious about that." Detective James gestured at the shambles of Sandy's apartment. "Me, I'd just like to know what's going on." James righted an overturned chair by Sandy's small dining table, patted the top of the chair back. "Make yourself to home."

Sandy sat down.

James picked up another chair and sat in front of him, leaned on his knees and gazed up at Sandy.

"Am I under arrest?" Sandy asked.

James inhaled, pursing his lips. "If you were still in New York, you would be. With me?" He glanced around at the room. "Not yet, but we're getting there."

The same species of prevarication Sandy employed to fool his colleagues, playing pranks on them, served now in concocting a plausible account of events. He'd gone to visit his friend in New York, he told James. After a day spent sight-seeing, he'd returned to Gordon's apartment and found him murdered. In the garage he'd overheard the killers arguing explicitly about what they'd done and he'd chased them, but they'd gotten away. He described the two men.

"Why didn't you go to the police?"

"I wasn't thinking straight. I've never seen someone murdered before. Maybe it was paranoia but I got the feeling I was being watched. I got scared. I mean, obviously these are determined people. I just wanted to get out of there. I was going to call when I got home."

"Mm-hm. Well, you're home. Looks like those people are interested in you too. What are they looking for, do you think?"

Sandy shook his head. "I don't know. They went through my things in Gordon's apartment, too. I'm guessing they got my name from my plane ticket. But I don't know what they were looking for. It looked like they'd tried to get into Gordon's safe. Gordon was an estate assessor for Sotheby's. Maybe he'd discovered evidence of fraud. This—" Sandy gestured around his apartment—"this is just mean. I can't explain it."

Sandy took a risk in the tale he'd told. At some point investigative efforts would lead to Arthur, Gordon's contact in the CCTV surveillance division, and they would see video of Sandy in Union Square, a full day before flight records showed he'd arrived in New York. Hopefully, that would happen later rather than sooner.

James tapped his cupped fingers together. "Okay, I'm not going to pretend I think that's the whole story. But from what I see here, your life has been violated enough for one day. So, I'm going to let you think about things, and ask you to come see me tomorrow, and we're going to have this conversation again." He straightened and gave Sandy his card. "Do not make me look for you."

"I understand. Thank you, Detective."

"As of now, your apartment is a material crime scene in an interstate homicide investigation. I'm going to allow you, under the supervision of my officers here, to gather some clothes and whatever you need to take yourself to a hotel or wherever you want to go, provided you do not leave the city. Then you're going to have to vacate your apartment until our investigators finish in here. You will inform us where you are when you're settled."

"All right."

"I want you to think real hard about what you're going to tell me tomorrow, Mister Creaze. You won't help anyone by withholding information."

Sandy didn't respond. The detective left the apartment.

The two uniformed officers stood by the door. Sandy stared about at the ruin of his home. Layer by layer, his old life was being taken from him, at the same time that he let it go. He felt like he didn't know himself anymore. Emotionally he was exhausted. The passion he felt for Lark, and his concern for her, was a dull ache. He'd overdosed on adrenaline and it was taking its toll, his ardor diminishing as concern for himself reasserted.

He threw a couple of shirts and changes of socks and underwear in a garbage bag with a few toiletries that were still usable, and left the wreckage behind.

He checked into the Crowne Plaza at LAX with a credit card, called from his room the number James had given him and reported his whereabouts. He called his boss and left word that he was quitting his job.

Then he drove down Lincoln Boulevard, looking for a cheap motel. He stopped at a 7-11 and bought a few pre-packaged sandwiches and bottled drinks. The inaccurately named Sea Crest Inn seemed accommodatingly innocuous; he checked in there, paying cash for two nights' stay. He had no intention of speaking with Detective James again. He lay on the bed in the small room, thinking he must be a fool to let himself be dragged so far from his comfortable, steady life by a kiss.

CHAPTER NINE

He stayed in the room, enduring the hours until it was time to go to the mall. He didn't want to risk being spotted, out and about. He got several calls from James on his cell phone, but ignored them.

Neither did he answer any of the calls he received from friends and co-workers. No doubt a lot of concern had been generated, as word of the break-in at his apartment and him quitting his job spread. He didn't like being a source of worry for others, and missed his friends. He didn't have anything to say to them. He couldn't imagine how to conduct a conversation with anyone, right then.

He questioned elliptically what he was doing, little room though he had in himself for doubts.

The Hierophant had been such a bizarre creature, Sandy could hardly credit his memory of the encounter. The boy who'd died and turned to ash was a scar on his mind. How could he put faith in the ways of a being so lethal and devoid of emotion?

He thought, too, of Lark, examined his feelings for her again and again. Many times he had ended relationships with women because the inconveniences in continuing with them seemed too great. If they lived too far apart, worked too often at conflicting hours, differed too greatly in their tastes, he would try for awhile but then get tired and let go. One brief night with Lark and he was throwing his life away.

But, God, what a night. The enthralling flush of passion had passed. But that moment, in bed with her, laughing, so connected, so at *home*, was too pure to sully with misgivings.

Still, as the hours dragged on, his resolve was tested. The motel room became claustrophobic. He grew irritated, angry, with the unfairness of the situation. Why should his last moments in the city he loved be restricted to four dingy walls and a lumpy bed?

The Hierophant had painted a dismal picture of his future, if he turned away from the door he had supposedly opened. Supposedly. Purportedly. There was no way of knowing what would occur when he followed that eldritch creature's instructions.

But he had to know.

More than anything, that need barred retreat. More even than his love for Lark. The universe had presented him with a chance to see beyond a veil. He had only one life that he knew of. If he turned away from the road before him, questions would haunt him to the end of his days:

What might he have learned? What might his life have become?

And then again, not more than love. He knew the brain science, the chemicals released by a body in the flush of attraction. That did not eliminate the impact of choice. It was always in the purview of the person to wait, let the chemical storm pass, postpone acting until the desire to do so expired. He had waited before until it was too late. He knew the texture of that choice like an old shirt.

By choice he called up the vision of Lark; by choice he bathed himself, his mind, his being, in the biological truth of love, and by that choice knew that what he felt and what drew him was greater than biology. Biology was an aftershock. Lark knelt beside him in his mind and he knew that she had awakened his soul.

The time arrived to go to the mall. Sandy didn't bother packing a bag. He showered and dressed and left the rest of his clothes in the motel room.

Driving out of the narrow parking lot, he spotted Detective James driving in. The two locked eyes and Sandy gunned his car onto the street, narrowly avoiding a bus that slammed on its breaks. He burned rubber up Lincoln Boulevard.

The bus blocked James from following. Sandy turned on La Tijera and took the access road to the mall. He parked in the underground lot and ran up the escalator, walked quickly to the spot where Lark and he had kissed.

He remembered the exact place where they had stood. His body knew it like a visceral landmark.

He stood, waiting and watching, checking the time on his phone. The minutes dragged like hours.

He didn't know the exact moment when he'd met Lark, but he knew it was drawing near. With dismay, he saw James hurrying toward him up the concourse. He didn't know how the man had located him. His phone, he realized. He was an idiot. They'd tracked him by his cell phone.

There was no point in running, no place to run to. The Hierophant had told him that he had to be in this place, at this moment, for the door to open.

James saw that Sandy wasn't running and slowed his gait. He put his hand on the chest of the uniformed officer with him, forestalling him seizing Sandy.

"Mr. Creaze, I told you not to make me look for you."

A hopelessness came over Sandy. He didn't respond.

"Your story doesn't add up. You know that. I'm going to have to ask you to come with me and explain yourself."

"Can we wait here, just for a moment?"

James frowned. He started to respond but his features became fixed, his mouth half open, framing an answer he never voiced.

Sandy blinked at him. "Detective James?"

The officer accompanying James too seemed immobilized. With increasing uneasiness, Sandy glanced around and saw that everyone in the mall had become frozen in place, caught in mid step, many with one foot suspended.

Goosebumps cascaded over his flesh. James' features softened with a gelatinous sheen. A black ooze exuded not so much from his skin as the dimensions of his presence, as if another reality were asserting itself. Color drained from everything—the floor, walls, ceiling, storefronts, everything seeping with an oozing blackness.

The walls acquired the character of slick, black stone, and the people around Sandy lost their distinguishing features, immersed in the same blackness, retaining only a generic semblance of human forms. A pulsing, siren screech split the air and the walls shifted and expanded, until Sandy found himself in a great, black cavern that extended right and left beyond the range of sight as an immense tunnel. The people lost cohesion, melting and slumping to the ground, oozing together and spilling into a deep channel that opened in the cavern floor. The wall to Sandy's right drew close, pressed against him until he was clinging to a narrow ledge on the verge of an oily river of bodies from which arose a collective moan.

On the far side of that river a faint light beckoned.

PART TWO

THE LAIR OF RAPTUROUS DELIGHTS

CHAPTER TEN

The ledge barely gave perch to his heels. Arms wide, palms flat against the wall, Alexander searched desperately for more secure footing.

The blackened bodies poured by in a horrid flood, forming a river so vast Sandy doubted he could have crossed it had it been made of water. It gave off noxious fumes that reeked of sulfur and rot. The bodies mimicked ripples and waves, merged indistinguishably in their flow.

The upper reaches of the cavernous tunnel were too distant, in the dim light, for him to discern their limit. The black walls glistened, smooth and irregular. The light that limned them had no discernible source.

The bead of light across the river still beckoned. It illumined a broad terrace fronting the entrance of a cave. Sandy wished he could will himself there. He dreaded losing himself to the eldritch river, becoming a molecule in its volume, stripped of will and identity.

He spied a slight widening of the ledge, thirty feet or so to his right, edged towards it, but then saw that the intervening span narrowed to barely an inch, and above the thinnest stretch the wall bulged outward. His legs trembling, he reversed course. Whether from despair or weakness, he fell into the river.

He screamed and thrashed, groped for the ledge but couldn't reach it. He tried to scramble across the bodies but they were too slick. Whatever he tried to hold slipped from his grasp, and his feet couldn't find purchase. His hand plunged down, encountered an icy chill. He managed to pull it out; his fingers and forearm stung in the open air. He struggled with increased frenzy. His feet slipped into the morass of bodies and he couldn't free them. The harder he groped for escape, the deeper he sank into the river's embrace. He slid in to his knees, his waist, crying, "No! No! No!" went in to his neck. His body numbed in the river's coldness. Only his face remained un-submerged, upturned. He breathed in short, desperate gulps.

The moans and murmurs were louder, close to his ears, their tenor despairing. Sandy was so cold he thought his heart would stop. Some instinct told him to quit resisting. He closed his eyes and went limp, expecting to be pulled under. The flowing bodies, pressing against him with awful sensuousness, pushed him upwards. It took all of his will to suppress panic. Gradually the river extruded him, shivering and panting, onto its surface.

He vomited and lay still a long while, afraid to move, his heart pounding. The oily flesh he rode was repellent. Even breathing through his mouth he tasted the vapors.

His position in relation to the node of light had not altered, but he was a few yards farther from the wall with the narrow ledge. The bodies slipped under him without carrying him along in their movement.

He found that by rolling his shoulders and thighs he could change his orientation to the current. He angled his feet toward the near wall. The motion of bodies slipping under him drew him toward it. He angled himself the opposite direction. For a long time it seemed the node of light drew no closer, but his distance from the wall he'd fallen from increased.

He let his head drop back and closed his eyes, surrendered to the slow journey, prayed that he would not wind up becalmed unto death. He saw the same scene with his eyes closed that he did with them open. Either way, the cavern yawned above him.

He tried to comfort himself with memories—people, experiences, features of the world—but the imagery his mind supplied was pale and fragmentary, shredded with voids the cavern claimed. He gave up and let it fill his mind.

Voices within the river's drone became transiently intelligible. They spoke in many languages; those Sandy understood voiced monolexical questions—*Why? When? Where? How?*

He thought of his humble home and longed for its comforts. He wanted his bed and the shelter of covers. He did not blame Lark, but wished he had never met her, or become so besotted that he'd thrown away his life. He had reached for a heroic quest and tumbled into a chasm of hell. The enormity of his isolation pressed down on him. He would die alone in this terrible place with no one to mourn his passing.

A pale form coalesced, levitating above him, and resolved into the figure of Lark. She wore white, flowing robes, and possessed the same glow that she had in their bedroom amid the stars. She smiled down at him.

"My love," Sandy whispered. Her smile broadened and he was comforted.

The vision faded and Sandy realized that his eyes were open. He looked around but she was gone.

His feet touched something hard. He had arrived at the far embankment. He scooted his upper body into alignment with it, carefully reached up and seized a rock protrusion. He rolled against the embankment and pulled himself onto the terrace.

He lay for a moment, breathing, then screamed again, venting terror. He pushed himself to his knees and looked back across the black river. He saw no portal through which he might have entered this dark demesne. He'd been transported by means he didn't understand. Towards what end he couldn't guess, but it seemed the Hierophant had kept its word. How he might proceed from here in search of Lark Sandy had no idea.

She'd been with him, out there, in his moment of despair. He had no proof of it, but it felt true. The life he'd known was gone. All he had left was love and will and wilted curiosity. Somehow, he would find her.

He looked down at himself. The black oil of the river had not clung to him, small relief. The bead of light still hovered at the cave entrance. Sandy rose and straightened his shoulders, breathed deep and approached it.

The light seemed to levitate and have substance. He almost walked into it before realizing it was near—a fuzzy, softly glowing orb about the size of a baseball. It hung suspended at eye-level without support.

The orb chittered and drifted into the cave. Sandy guessed he was meant to follow. Past several bends in a narrow passage the way ahead shone with greater brilliance. The winding passage opened onto another enormous cavern, this one aglow with a golden light that emanated from the walls themselves.

The walls were carved with giant letters and symbols, each many times a man's height. Some were of alphabets and writing systems familiar to Sandy. He recognized Latin, Arabic, Cyrillic, Chinese and Sanskrit, but there were many more. There were also hieroglyphs and pictographs. Looking closer, he saw that each letter or symbol bore beneath it, carved small, an attribution. 'Herman Melville' was engraved beneath a giant 'C," James Joyce' beneath an 'S.' Other letters were attributed to Mary Anne Evans, Shakespeare and Boëthius.

"What *is* this place?" he murmured to himself.

The orb led him on and Sandy followed, staring about in awe. The cavern seemed endless.

They came upon an opening in the right hand wall, beneath the Chinese symbol for 'branch,' attributed to Wang Wei, and Sandy followed the orb into another passage. Beyond, past another long bend, they entered a humbler cavern with stalactites and stalagmites and flowstone walls. The walls here did not glow. By some distant light the mineral formations cast long shadows.

The orb led him toward the light. As they drew near, Sandy heard voices.

Chapter Eleven

The place appeared to be a bar.

Through a flowstone archway, Sandy looked in on a sprawling establishment with hundreds of round-topped tables arranged among mineral columns, and a long bar at the far inner limit.

The clientele were even more bizarre in their attire than had been those in the underground club Lark had taken him to in New York. Several wore capes and leotards, like fantasy superheroes, though without the masks or distinguishing markers that might identify them specifically. A number were dressed in the manners of warriors of cultures both ancient and contemporary. Some were naked, or wore only minimal clothing. Some possessed extraordinary physical beauty, others were grotesquely deformed, among the latter a person who possessed no skin at all. Some seemed to be incompletely formed, their features hazy. A man wearing a smoking jacket and an ascot had his head wrapped in bandages.

Sandy leaned back and read the sign carved above the archway: *Le Cabaret d'Archétypes*.

A red rope extended across the entrance. On the other side a big man in a baseball jersey and cap sat on a stool talking to a tall man dressed in a grass skirt and extravagant headdress. The tall man nodded toward Sandy and the man in the baseball get-up turned.

"Sorry," he said. "Password?"

Sandy remembered the word Lark had used in New York. He didn't know if it would work here. He wasn't sure, either, that he wanted to engage with the people in this place.

The man in the baseball uniform craned forward, waiting.

"Ramshackle," Sandy said.

The man unclipped the rope and swept his hand out for Sandy to enter. Sandy felt a nudge at his shoulder; the orb chittered quietly. It wanted him to go in. Still Sandy hesitated, until his eyes fixed on the bartender at the distant bar.

The noise of conversation in many languages grew louder as he crossed the threshold, as if he penetrated an invisible barrier.

"… don't want anything to do with that …"

"I remember …"

"… time to ask that question …"

He advanced through the room, aware of scrutiny. The din of talk quieted. He strode to the bar.

The bartender met his gaze.

Sandy marshaled his emotions. "Appox," he said.

Appox's eyebrows rose. "It's good to see you again, sir."

"Gonna throw me out?"

Appox seemed surprised. "You are a member in good standing."

"How's that?"

Appox shrugged. "You are here."

Sandy inhaled sharply, squinting at Appox. "There's a couple of thousand damn questions I have to ask."

"I'll answer as best I can. Would you like a drink? Durach's Own, as I recall."

Sandy clenched and unclenched his hands at his sides. He sensed no evasion from Appox. He relaxed his shoulders and nodded. Appox took a bottle from the mirror-backed shelves behind the bar. Sandy noticed his own reflection with shock. He looked twenty years younger.

Appox poured him a drink. Sandy downed half of it in a gulp and closed his eyes, letting the liquor work its way to his nerves. He peered again at his reflection. There was something on his jacket. He looked down at himself. The breast now bore a woven emblem, like a coat of arms.

He took another deep breath. "Where the hell *am* I?"

Appox frowned faintly. "You're in the Archetypes' Club."

Sandy shook his head impatiently. "I read the sign. I was in Los Angeles and now I'm here. Where the hell is here?"

Appox's frown deepened. "You're in … the Labyrinth."

Sandy squeezed his eyes shut. "Oh, good." He stretched them open and blinked several times. "Let's try for how did I *get* here?"

A man on a nearby stool said, "You quickened here, pal. It's the only way *to* get here." The man looked like he'd walked out of an old movie. He wore a dark grey trench-coat and a black fedora.

"I don't know how to do that or even what it *means*."

"He must have lost his memory," said a female voice behind him.

Sandy looked back to discover that the clientele of the bar had gathered around him. He couldn't identify the speaker. "My memory is just fine."

"What's your name?" said an obese woman sprawled on a levitating divan. By her voice Sandy knew she was not the one who had spoken before.

He stared at her a beat, trying to work out how she stayed aloft. "Alexander Creaze. Sandy for short," he answered distractedly. River of dead people, guy with no skin, floating fat woman—the new normal.

"Well, if you didn't quicken, how *did* you get here?" asked a man with narrow, Asian features and a long goatee. He wore an iridescent charcoal grey robe and a tall, black lacquer hat with long, stiff wings.

Sandy sensed no aggression from the people before him, only interest. There seemed no reason not to answer. "I sort of slid across a river of corpses and walked."

A gasp went through the crowd.

The man in the fedora said, "You gave someone a coin, didn't you?"

Sandy sucked his teeth. "A, uh … *person* calling itself the Hierophant."

More gasps ensued.

"The Quints brought him to the club in New York," Appox said. "She presented him as Knight-errant."

This information seemed to both astonish and delight the odd gathering. Sandy fired Appox a sharp look. "Finish the story." He turned to the crowd and cocked his head back at Appox. "He shot her. With a gun."

Shock, now, as eyes turned to Appox.

"It was an accident," he said. "Garritch quickened into the bar and cast a pall on her. I tried to eject him but failed. He shimmered and my bullet went through him and hit the Quints. Garritch quickened out of the bar with her before I could intervene."

The onlookers fell into animated conversation.

"Hey," Sandy called out. "Hey!" When he had their attention again, he said, "How about somebody tell me what's going on?"

The man in the fedora said, "Looks like you've stumbled into a fight."

"That's one hell of a stumble, Bogie," said the levitating fat woman.

"I've asked you not to call me that, Crisis," the man in the fedora answered her. "Why don't we all ease up and let me talk to this man. I'll fill everyone in when we're done."

The onlookers drifted apart and Sandy followed the man in the fedora to a secluded table where Appox joined them. The man in the fedora signaled someone else. A tall and startlingly beautiful woman with long blond hair came over and joined them as well. She was naked except for a clamshell covering her vulva.

"Sandy, I'm Sam," said the man in the fedora. "Appox you know, and this is Virgin."

Sandy, brought up old school, stood partway to greet Virgin, keeping his groin concealed by the table.

"It isn't you, it's me," she said, smiling and sitting down. "I have that effect on most men, regardless of their sexual orientation."

Sandy reddened and cleared his throat. "Oh … ah," was all he managed, with an embarrassed grin.

The glowing orb drifted over and hovered by his left shoulder. His tablemates reacted with surprise.

"You have a Wander with you?" Virgin asked.

"I … don't know what that is. The thing was waiting for me on this side of the black river. It led me here."

Sam gave the Wander a scrupulous look. "Tell us more about how you got here. We'll do our best to help you."

Sandy sniffed and looked around the room at the menagerie of bizarre characters, watched an elderly woman in an anachronistically elegant evening gown drain a glass of champagne. He didn't know what to make of the three at his table, but it was good to have people to talk to. They said they wanted to help; he supposed he could do worse than give them a chance.

He told Appox, Sam and Virgin how he had met Lark, and summarized events that had transpired since. When he finished, his three companions regarded each other with shared concern.

"We're going to have another time slip," Appox said. "It will have less of an impact, restricted to the Labyrinth."

"The portals here are locked?" Sam asked.

Appox nodded. "They can get in other ways."

"There's a question of who's with whom," Virgin said quietly, glancing around.

"Hey, people," Sandy interrupted, "feels like I'm coming in at the end of a long damn conversation."

"Sorry, Sandy," Sam said. "Like I said, you've stumbled into a fight."

"More like a war," Virgin said.

Sandy planted a fingertip on the table. "I stumbled into love, nothing else. My concern is to find Lark. Whatever intrigue you all have going on is none of my business."

"The Hierophant would not approach a bystander," Virgin said. "He would not have accepted your coin."

"That thing is a *he?*"

Virgin smiled faintly. "He is a bit … androgynous, but yes. He is also beyond definition, and a terrible force within nature. He keeps secrets many of us don't want to know. But he is a defender of the Labyrinth and the Traveling Doors, and would not involve you for no purpose."

Sandy sat back and stared at Virgin, saw past her nudity to the person schooling him. "You people fucking excel at talking in riddles." He downed more Scotch and wiped his mouth. "Look, I'll do what I have to. But the Hierophant's purpose and mine are not the same thing. For starters he didn't clue me in about his, so I'm not feeling beholden to *him*. That Garritch character abducted Lark," he aimed a finger at Appox, "right out from under your nose. Nobody gets to reset my priorities, and number one is seeing her safe."

"The Quints isn't who you think she is," Sam said.

"Nobody tells me who that woman is. What passed between us was real. It still is."

Sam shook his head. "I said that badly. I'm not doubting you, Sandy. There are things about her you don't know. The Quints is a big deal down here."

"She's the Keeper of the Five Ways," Appox said. "The stability of the Traveling Doors depends on her."

Sandy lowered his gaze at Appox. "Still not understanding."

Appox studied Sandy a moment. "At the core of the situation is the fabric of reality. Some want freedom and openness. That would include the three of us here at this table with you. Some want to define the future, and make themselves its sole architects. Of the latter, Garritch, in this realm, is the prime mover. There may be other, elder beings manipulating him of whom we are ignorant. He abducted the Quints because he wants to control her. He wants to be the keeper of keys."

Sandy grimaced in frustration. "So he's an evil son-of-a-bitch, got that. How do I find him and fuck up his shit?"

Virgin burst out laughing and Sam smiled crookedly.

Appox, taken aback, glanced at the others in confusion. "Alexander, these are serious matters, not to be taken lightly."

"The love of my life has been kidnapped," Sandy snapped, "my friend murdered, my apartment ransacked, my entire life stripped from me like it never existed, I've crossed a river of melting corpses to arrive in Weirdsville and be told that the fate of the fucking cosmos is at risk, and I'm trying to keep my brain from exploding and surrendering to the likely conclusion that I've gone profoundly nuts. In what way do you imagine I'm not serious?"

Sandy's companions sobered.

"We can't tell you how to get to Garritch," Sam said. "He's hiding somewhere and he's good at it. He's powerful; you've seen that yourself. He's a master of creating illusions, and there's no one better at summoning doors. We've only been able to guess his intentions from the effects of his actions."

"The Quints would not have chosen you frivolously," said Virgin. "She saw in you the qualities necessary to meet the challenges."

"She didn't choose me," Sandy said.

Appox, Sam and Virgin frowned in confusion.

"'You didn't pick me, and I didn't pick you; we found each other.' That's what she said. I remember with crystal clarity her every word." Sandy registered his companions' expressions. "What?"

"He doesn't know who he is," Virgin said to Appox.

Sandy goggled Virgin, shaking his head with his palms upraised. "Lady, I don't even know what that *means*."

"You're the Knight-errant, pal," Sam said, "the true and noble defender of the Five Ways. You hold allegiance to no code but your own."

"People keep saying that to me: 'You're the Knight-errant, you're the Knight-errant.' Again, no fucking comprendo."

"You're a living archetype," Appox said. "You have come to embody—unwittingly, evidently—a requirement in the field of consciousness."

Sandy laughed helplessly. "Pretending I have any *idea* what you're talking about, I am *telling* you I am no archetype. I have done *nothing* in my life so noteworthy that it would *make* me an archetype, and, not for nothing, I do not want to *be* an archetype."

A bearded man in a cape sitting at a nearby table overheard Sandy and bellowed with laughter. "Hey, everybody," he shouted, "guy here says he doesn't want to be an archetype!"

Others laughed, and the laughter spread until everyone in the bar was overcome with hilarity. Even Appox was infected. He tried to restrain himself but burst out laughing with the rest.

Sandy stared around in growing frustration. "Let me in on the fucking *joke!*" he shouted.

The fat woman on the levitating divan glided by. "No one does, boy!" she exclaimed and floated on, laughing with the rest.

Sandy crossed his arms and waited for the laughter to subside.

Sam sobered himself and gripped Sandy's forearm. "Everyone here is an archetype, pal. You can't get in if you're not."

CHAPTER TWELVE

Sandy wanted something to make sense the way that it used to. He recognized that Sam was sincere, but it didn't help. Then he found himself looking at Sam differently, at his fedora and trenchcoat, and the others, with their outlandish garb and characteristics, all seeming, in ways he couldn't pin down, distillations of *type*, and sensed an underlying truth in what he was being told. In this place some hidden principle was laid bare.

He noticed a woman standing across the room. She had long, auburn tresses and wore flowing, light brown robes. He doubted his eyes for a moment, then knew she was Lark.

He stood up, his chair falling behind him, and strode towards her.

"Sandy?" Sam called after him.

"Lark!" Sandy cried.

She turned at the sound of her name but showed no sign of recognition.

"Lark, it's me. Sandy."

Surprise spread on her face. She smiled uncertainly. "Do I know you?"

"More than *know*."

She shook her head. "I'm sorry, I don't—"

Appox grabbed Sandy and pulled him around. "She is not here by her own volition. The portals have been compromised."

Sandy pulled himself free and took Lark by the shoulders. "Lark—" he shook her gently—"it's me. We found each other, remember?" He took her wrist, lifted her hand, and lightly touched his fingertips to hers.

She stared in confusion. A series of expressions crossed her face and recognition arrived. "Sandy?"

He smiled. "I came for you. I'm here."

"Sandy!" She fell into his arms and he seized her in a tight embrace. The aching emptiness he'd felt was filled, and he groaned with relief. She was not a lie, not a figment of his imagination; she was *real*. He felt her love pour into him like a warm and healing wind.

Sam and Virgin came to their sides. "You two have to get out of here," Sam said.

"You're ensnared," Virgin told Lark. "I can see the web holding you."

Lark nodded. "He has me."

"Take her away if you can, Knight-errant," Virgin said to Sandy. "Protect her. She is more important than you can imagine."

A tremor passed through the floor. All talk ceased. The patrons of the Cabaret of Archetypes looked at each other with wariness. The tremor recurred, and the agitation of the archetypes increased. Many of those sitting stood up.

Appox loped through the club, scanning the walls. "Violation!" he shouted. "Prepare yourselves!"

"Come on," Sandy said, pulling Lark toward the entrance. But the entrance was gone. The archway was blocked by a flat, grey wall. Lark's hand pulled from his grasp. She stared at Sandy beseechingly. Her feet seemed stuck to the floor.

Sam grabbed Sandy's arm. "What did the Hierophant give you?"

"What?"

The tremors gained intensity. Bottles fell from shelves and glasses from tables. Cracks formed in the walls. Appox leapt over the bar and disappeared behind it.

"A weapon," Sam said. "He gave you a weapon!"

Sandy shook his head. "He didn't."

"He did," Sam said, shaking him. "What did he give you?"

Sandy remembered the vernier caliper. He patted his pockets, pulled it out. "He gave me this, see? Not a weapon—" The caliper changed, lengthening, unfolding, until it became a long, heavy sword, engraved with symbols the likes of which Sandy had never seen.

A terrible strength flooded into Sandy. The symbols on the sword glowed white and light blazed from the entire blade.

"Holy fuck!" he yelled.

"You *are* the Knight-errant," Virgin told him. She was now clad in chain mail of fine links form-fitting her figure. In her left hand she held a long halberd. A blue stone shone in the center of her forehead.

"You're going to have to fight for her, pal," Sam said. "Get your head straight. We need you."

"I'm not sure everyone here will stand with us," Virgin said.

"Watch your back," Sam told Sandy. He pulled a revolver from inside his coat. "Keep hold of your weapon."

The cracks widening in the walls oozed a black substance. Lark moaned. A network of cracks had formed directly under her. Ooze bled from them and sent tendrils snaking up her legs like a network of veins. She began to convulse and her eyes rolled back in her head.

Sandy seized her around her waist and tried to pull her free. The fat woman on the floating divan sailed towards him, laughing maniacally, electricity arcing from her hair. A force burst from the prow of her divan. Sam and Virgin were knocked to the ground. Sandy lost hold of the sword and it quickly folded back into its humbler state as an implement.

The fat woman leaned down and snatched it up. A shot rang out and a red wound opened in her side. Appox stood on top of the bar, holding a shotgun with a smoking barrel.

Crisis dropped the caliper, shouting, "Damn you, Appox!" and veered away.

Lark was sinking into the floor, pulled down by the black tendrils that now ensnared her up to her throat. Sandy held her desperately, straining to snag the caliper with his foot. He couldn't reach it. Sam wrapped his arms around Lark and pulled with Sandy, but she continued to sink.

The rest of the archetypes fell into conflict with each other, possessed, now, of even more fantastic attributes. The cracks in the walls widened, and oily black beings like those that had composed the black river emerged; glowing coals burned eye-like in their otherwise featureless faces. They bore weapons, mostly swords and lances, but a few had guns. With their arrival a foul odor entered the club.

"Ur-men," Sam snarled. "Garritch has raised the dead."

Sandy couldn't tell who was on whose side. Some of the archetypes engaged with the oily entities, some fought alongside them. Sam and Sandy began to lose their purchase on Lark. Her body was nearly covered with the black ooze. The ur-soldiers emerged in greater numbers from the walls. Sam had to let go of Lark to defend himself and she slipped from Sandy's grasp, vanishing into the floor.

"No!" Sandy groped at the floor where the cracks had closed.

"She's gone!" Sam kicked him. "Defend yourself! You're the only one who can save her!"

Virgin stood over the vernier caliper, guarding it, fighting both ur-men and fellow archetypes. Sandy dove for it but was attacked by a bearded, muscular, caped archetype bearing an enormous hammer. The archetype straddled Sandy, gripping his throat with one hand and raising the hammer to strike him with the other; Sandy seized the archetype's raised arm with both of his hands, preventing him from delivering the blow.

Gunfire, clashing steel and cries of conflict joined the rising din of the rumbling walls. Sandy pushed himself with his heels toward Virgin, who was bleeding from several wounds. He dragged the bearded brute with him, saw a chance, released the archetype's hammer-wielding arm and reached for the caliper, straining his head aside as the hammer came down, barely avoiding getting his head crushed. The hammer grazed the side of his head and tore his ear.

Sandy shouted in pain but got hold of the caliper. It transformed again and its power flowed through him. With a roar he threw off his attacker and rose to his feet. A further transformation occurred: a metal glove unfolded on his hand, and more metal unfolded farther, piecing together from invisible particles, up his arm, around his neck, and on, until his entire body was armored. The hammer-wielder backed away, hand raised to shield his face.

Sandy took in the chaos around him. The air grew thick with smoke; the odors of cordite and gunpowder mixed with the foulness of rot. The picture reflected in the mirror behind the bar was a surrealist vision of hell. Sam spun, fanning his pistol, his coat flaring out as he turned. A giant with a face like a jumble of obsidian swung a stone chair into a cluster of ur-soldiers so hard that the chair broke. Three of the soldiers didn't get back up. The giant was left holding one of the chair legs, which he proceeded to wield as a club. Appox still stood atop the bar, firing his shotgun. The old Asian man leapt into the air and countered both bullets and steel with his fan, dispatched two ur-men and a fellow archetype clad like a soldier of ancient Rome.

The strength that poured through Sandy conveyed to him confidence and clarity; uncertainty about his capacity for battle was swept from his being. Lark was being used against him. He faced his foes and the thought burst in his mind: *Bring it.*

Ur-soldiers continued to pour into the bar. About a third of the archetypes seemed to align with them. Sandy fought his way toward Virgin. Two ur-soldiers confronted him and he decapitated both with a swipe of his blade; fountains of black ichor sprouted from their necks.

Virgin was cut on her legs and arms and she'd been shot in the shoulder, but fought like she felt no pain. The main mass of attackers pressed in Sandy's direction. Allies drew to him and fought at his sides. Sam's pistol must have possessed magical attributes, like Sandy's sword, for he never seemed to need to reload it. The same seemed true of Appox's shotgun. Sandy lost cognizance of archetype and ur-man. He fought those who attacked him and his allies, merciless in his blows. He gave himself to the intelligence of his body, ducked, dodged, swung and stabbed without thought, focused on battle.

The floor grew slick, black and red with blood. Still the walls shook and ur-soldiers poured through the cracks. The defenders of the bar were increasingly outnumbered. A knot of them formed a ring of defense with Sandy, among them the Chinese fan wielder, the skinless man, the obsidian giant, Appox, Sam and Virgin.

Appox fired repeatedly at the wall that blocked the club entrance and blew a hole in it. He kept firing, increasing the hole's size, and Sandy and his allies fought toward it. The dead and wounded littered the floor.

The rumbling ceased and a siren screech tore the air. Fighters on both sides were arrested in their struggles. A crack formed in the ceiling and a segment gave way, crashing down on a cluster of ur-men beneath it. A figure in a long, black, embroidered coat floated down through the opening to stand on the fallen stone disc. His eyes were closed. They opened and fixed on Sandy.

Garritch stepped down from the stone disc and the ur-soldiers and their allied archetypes made way. He came nimbly over the fallen toward Sandy, smiled and raised his hands like a conductor. Sandy felt a hideous force assail him and his own strength diminish in its path. His sword remained intact but his armor disintegrated.

"You shall not cast in this place!" Appox yelled, and fired at Garritch. Garritch jerked his head and the shotgun blast diverted, hitting one of his ur-soldiers.

Sandy raised his sword; he would not go down meekly. Garritch looked contemptuous, but then the confidence in his expression faltered.

The Wander hovered by Sandy's side. A stream of energy, invisible except for the rippling distortion it caused in the air, issued from it at Garritch. The stream gave off tremendous heat. Sandy and those nearest moved away from it. Garritch gestured frantically, trying to ward off the attack. His coat caught fire, his face was scalded and his hair began to smoke. He cried out in rage and vanished.

A shockwave radiated from the place where he'd stood, knocking all in its path to the floor.

The ur-soldiers, both animate and slain, withdrew and were drawn back through the cracks in the walls from which they had issued. The cracks re-sealed and only the archetypes remained. The wall blocking the entrance to the club vanished.

Sandy's sword collapsed into a caliper. He stared about in horror at the dead.

Chapter Thirteen

Archetypes who had moments before been fighting each other joined in tending the wounded. The dead were lined up against a wall, shrouded with tablecloths. Sandy helped as he could until the work that remained fell to those with medical knowledge. He returned to the table he'd sat at with Sam and Virgin and stared about numbly. A baseball cap rested on one of the shrouded bodies. Sandy watched Appox lay a bandage over the wound he had himself inflicted in the levitating fat woman's abdomen.

The Wander, hovering by Sandy's left shoulder, warbled softly. Sandy understood kinesthetically that it conveyed empathy.

A robust, grey-haired archetype with a full beard came to the table bearing a beer and a glass of whiskey. He wore eyeglasses and a khaki vest. He sat down and placed the whiskey in front of Sandy.

"Appox says that's your poison."

Sandy watched the man sip his beer and grimace.

"Not good?"

The man shrugged. "It's what didn't get shot. It's wet."

Sandy turned his vernier caliper on the table, bewildered by its mysteries. He quit fiddling with it and placed his hand around the whisky glass but didn't drink. "I don't understand."

His companion sighed.

"Which side were you on?"

"You think there were sides?"

Sandy met his gaze.

"I fought for you and the Quints and the freedom of the Traveling Doors," the grey-haired man said.

Sandy sipped his Scotch. Among all the mysteries it might never have tasted so good.

The orb warbled, differently than before.

"Do you understand what it's saying?" he asked his tablemate.

The man cocked an eye at the orb. "She says we're not archetypes."

Sandy frowned at the man and the orb. It warbled some more.

"She says that's a common misconception—what people think we are."

"It's a she?"

The man nodded and the orb warbled again.

"She says real archetypes are things the significance of which we don't fully understand."

The orb changed shape, taking on the appearance of several geometric figures in succession: a circle, a six-, then twelve-sided star, a trapezoid, an equilateral triangle.

"I don't know what to do," Sandy said.

"About what?"

"She was here, in my arms, pleading for help, and I couldn't save her. Now she's gone again, and I've become a killer."

The man didn't respond for a moment. Then he said, "Why don't you quit?"

Sandy glared at him, anger rising in his chest. The man returned his regard impassively.

Sandy threw back his Scotch, shoved the vernier caliper in a pocket and stood up, retaining eye-contact with the grey-haired stranger. "Not likely," he said.

The grey-haired man chuckled and raised his glass.

Sam and Virgin were helping the old Asian man into a chair. The latter had his left arm in a sling. Virgin was naked again, bandaged in several places. Sam seemed unscathed. His fedora had a tear in its brim.

"I'm going after Lark," Sandy told them.

Virgin smiled, raising her chin. The respect in her eyes lifted Sandy.

"Never doubted you for a second, pal," Sam said.

"Can either of you help?"

Virgin nodded at Appox. "He can."

Appox was still tending Crisis. He pinched her eyelids open with his thumb, one after the other, peering in her eyes, then checked the bandage on her prodigious belly. "Drink plenty of fluids," he told her, "by which I mean *water*, and stay away from spicy and greasy foods for awhile, if you can manage it."

Crisis saw Sandy and grinned at him wryly. Appox turned.

"I should be going," Sandy told him.

Appox wagged two fingers toward the bar. "Come with me."

Sandy, Virgin and Sam followed him.

"Nothing you know from the life you knew will help you. Not in any way you're accustomed to." Appox led them behind the bar and pulled open a trap door in the floor. They followed him down a flight of stairs into a cellar. "Memories can be an impediment."

"What do you mean?"

Appox opened his medical kit and began to swab Sandy's wounded ear.

Sandy flinched away. "Leave it."

"Stop being foolish and hold still." Appox swabbed away blood. "Memories have a lot in common with dreams." He threaded a curved needle. "Both are slippery and open to interpretations that may or may not be valid." He started stitching closed the tear where the helix of Sandy's ear joined the skin of his temple.

Sandy winced and gritted his teeth. Appox was deft with the needle.

"Why do I remember something? Why did I dream that dream?" Appox asked rhetorically. "Both can be looked at as my mind tossing things up to help me or get in my way, which can be the same thing." He snipped the thread and started preparing a bandage.

"Don't cover the ear. I need my hearing."

Appox laid a strip of gauze behind Sandy's ear. "In the Labyrinth it's better to think of memories as a kind of conversation you're having with yourself." He taped the bandage in place. "I can't explain it better than that. Just bear it in mind."

Appox closed his medical kit and went to a small desk in a corner of the cellar. He shuffled through papers strewn upon it, found what he sought, which appeared to be a blank sheet, held it close to his lips and spoke words Sandy couldn't hear.

He held the paper out to Sandy. "Spit on it."

"What?"

"I believe I'm speaking your primary language. Spit on it."

Sandy widened his eyes, gave his head a shake and did as directed.

Appox crumpled the paper up and tossed it in the air. At the apex of its rise it snapped flat and floated back down.

"Catch it before it touches the floor," Appox said.

Sandy snatched the sheet from the air. It didn't show a single crease, nor the stain of his saliva. It was still blank on both sides. "What's this?"

"It's a map."

Sandy looked again. "It's blank."

"It is now. It doesn't have a context from which to guide you."

The Wander was still with Sandy. It warbled and Appox frowned at it.

"What did it say?" Sandy asked.

"She says you're likely to go places where a map won't help."

"Where am I going?"

"Into the Labyrinth," Appox said. "If you're going to find the Quints and free her from Garritch there's no other way. None that I know of."

"I thought we're in the Labyrinth."

"We are. It's all around us. It's a network of passage-ways, always changing. Some places within it are fixed. You can't quicken to where Garritch is—"

"Because I can't travel that way."

Appox shook his head. "You can quicken, Sandy. At some point you'll understand that. It isn't something that can be taught because nobody does it the same. But it wouldn't help you because Garritch is hiding and he'll have closed all the doors around him."

"You keep saying doors. What doors?"

"It's just a way of talking about quickening. They're all around us, like the Labyrinth. Once you understand how you do it you'll be able to summon a door and go from place to place. There's no way to accurately describe the passageways through the underside of consciousness. The Labyrinth is a back door to everywhere. I can't tell you what you'll run into out there. You can enter at any point and wind up at any other. Your intention to reach your objective is your surest guide."

Sandy shook his head and sighed. "Again with the riddles."

"Some matters defy clarification. With experience what I've told you will make more sense." Appox placed a hand on Sandy's shoulder. "There are forces aligned against you. They're going to try to confuse your path. It isn't the realm of *your* consciousness you've entered, it's everyone's and everything's. Forces that are entirely neutral to you and your purpose may simply be drawn to you in ways that may help or hinder. There are beings that live in the Labyrinth that have no interest whatsoever in the matters that concern us. It is a dangerous and uncertain place."

"So, what you're telling me, basically, is go in and follow my instincts until I find my way out."

"More or less."

"And that's all you can tell me."

Appox shrugged. "I can tell you lots of things about the Labyrinth but it won't do you any good and there isn't time. Just ask yourself, as you go along, if you're being diverted from your course. You'll make mistakes, but keep going. Anything that makes you feel like you can't is a lie. It's a deception. This will be as much a journey through yourself as it will a journey through a physical realm."

Sandy chuckled in frustration. "And you don't think you just contradicted yourself."

"I'm not trying to be immaculately consistent."

"So, where do I start?"

Appox gestured up toward the bar. "Where you came in." He sidled past Virgin and Sam and headed back up the stairs.

Virgin patted Sandy's arm. "We're coming with you."

Sam winked at him.

Sandy swallowed and nodded gratefully. He had been dreading being back on his own.

Back up behind the bar, Appox accepted three knapsacks from a barmaid and handed them to Sandy, Virgin and Sam. "Bread, cheese, fruit, salami, flasks of water. I don't know if it will last you until you get where you're going."

Sandy gave his knapsack to Sam. "Let me have a minute with Appox, I need to tell him something."

"We'll wait for you by the entrance," Virgin said, and they left.

"My friend who was killed," Sandy said, "I think you knew him."

Appox's eyebrows rose.

"His name was Gordon Cumberland. He met you here in the bar." Sandy looked around uncertainly. "Or *a* bar, some other version of this one, maybe. But he met you in what was for him a dream. A long time ago. At least for him—you don't seem to have aged as he had. Something happened, there was an altercation—people forcing their way in—and you did something, *pushed* Gordon out, and he woke up in a different place than where he'd gone to sleep."

Appox frowned in thought.

"I think you gave him a coin."

Appox's eyes widened with recognition. "Stillwater."

"What?"

"That's what we called him here, Stillwater. Yes, I remember. The Miner's Brawl. Stillwater was a dream walker. They're very rare. Was it his coin you gave Cabal?"

"Yes."

Sadness overcame Appox. "He's dead?"

"I'm sorry, yes. When I described you to him, he remembered you. With affection."

"He was a kind person. A deep soul." Appox's expression darkened. "Who killed him?"

"I don't know who they were. A tall, skinny white guy with a hat, and a short black guy built like a wrestler. They wanted the coin."

"Gadfly and Slick." Appox's eyes narrowed sidelong. "I'll be holding a grudge against them for that."

Chapter Fourteen

Appox and Sandy met Sam and Virgin at the entrance of the bar. Sandy noticed the Wander still with him. "You coming too?"

The Wander warbled and he didn't need a translator.

"What is this thing?" he asked his companions. "Is it—*she*—a guide?"

Appox eyed the Wander. "I wouldn't count on that."

The Wander chittered sharply.

"What did she say?"

"She reminded me that it was she who expelled Garritch from the bar—"

The Wander chittered some more.

"—and told me to mind my own business," Appox translated. "Remember what I said, Sandy. Trust your own instincts."

Sandy peered into the cave outside. "Any last words of wisdom?"

Appox shook his head.

Everyone in the bar was watching them. In the eyes of most, Sandy saw hope and encouragement. Surprisingly,

Crisis was among the latter. In others he saw uncertainty, reserve, fear, ambivalence. The grey-haired stranger raised his beer.

Sandy shook Appox's hand. He couldn't think of anything more to say either. Sam gave him a nod and Virgin winked at him. Without further ado, they departed.

Immediately they crossed the threshold their surroundings changed radically. They found themselves in a colossal cavern with luminous walls. The ground was ribbed with flowstone, the ceiling, so distant its height was unguessable, crowded with stalactites.

"Anything familiar?" he asked his companions.

"Not really," Sam said.

Virgin shook her head. To Sandy's relief, she was now clad in a khaki jumpsuit.

Sandy took out the map and unfolded it.

"Anything?" Sam asked.

"Blank." Sandy showed him.

The Wander drifted right, into the cavern, and warbled at them. Sandy gestured at it and shrugged: "I guess."

They followed the Wander, passing among pools of still water, some of which steamed.

"Have either of you traveled through the Labyrinth before, or have you just done the quickening thing?" Sandy asked.

"Not blind, like this," Sam said.

"In my early days here, I did," said Virgin. "I was a Discalced Carmelite Nun before I discovered that I was Quick. I traveled these realms extensively, finding myself."

Sandy glanced at her. "Is that why you're called Virgin?"

She smiled. "Everyone wants to know if I've kept my vows."

"I didn't mean—"

"It's all right," Virgin shook her head. "It isn't a driving force in my life anymore. Knowing what I know now unburdened me of many notions. My faith, though, the core of it, remains intact. But I am not the person I was."

"I was a cop in New York," Sam said. "Drew a case. Home invasion, bad as it gets. I won't describe it. It was connected to this, though."

"It was? How?"

"That black stuff the dead men are made of, it doesn't exist on Earth. It was in that house, though. He'd made them drink it."

"Why?"

"I don't know. I think it was some kind of experiment. Almost caught the son-of-a-bitch, chasing him through an abandoned warehouse in Brooklyn. I'm looking right at him and, poof, he vanishes. I was in motion, running like he was still there—my head hadn't made sense of it. Found myself in Tokyo, which took some adjustment."

"Did you catch him?" Sandy asked.

"Not yet."

Sandy glanced at Virgin. "How did you …" He didn't know how to finish his question.

"Find out that I'm one of the Quick?"

He nodded.

"I was in the cloister, holding a solitary all-night vigil, praying in the chapel." She glanced around. "I found myself in a much bigger church."

The cavern's far reaches never seemed to draw nearer. The trio lost track of time. They stopped to eat by the foot of a mineral column as big around as a house.

Sandy stared up at it, drinking water from his flask. He lifted his chin at the Wander. "Any idea where she's taking us?"

His companions shook their heads.

"Tell me about summoning doors."

"I just think where I want to go," Sam said.

Virgin smiled. "Sam is reductive to a fault. For me it's more of a ritual. I make the sign of the cross, and say a short prayer."

"And think where you want to go?"

Virgin nodded.

"Could either of you quicken us out of here?"

"Sure," Sam said, "But we have to follow your lead."

"If I told you to take us someplace else, though, wouldn't it be doing that?"

"Where do you want to go?" Virgin asked.

Home, Sandy thought, staring into the cavern. Not any home he'd known—a place where he could rest his head on Lark's chest and listen to her beating heart. "I don't know."

"There you are," said Sam.

Sandy pulled out his map.

"Anything?" Sam asked.

Sandy shook his head. They moved on. The cant of the cavern veered left and the way grew increasingly steep. They had to rest more frequently. Time passed without measure. The floor leveled out and sloped downwards, and still the cavern seemed endless.

"*Where* the hell *are* we?" Sandy asked in exasperation. "Where *is* this place?"

"There are scholars who spend their lives trying to answer that question," Virgin replied.

"Oh come on, are we inside the Earth? What?"

"Where is Earth?" Sam said.

Sandy threw his hands up. "It's in the solar system, in the Milky Way Galaxy, in the Universe."

"And where is the Universe?"

"In *space. Fuck!* I don't know. We know where things are in relation to other things. Where is this place in relation to the Earth?"

"It's hard to say."

Sandy groaned. "You guys."

"We don't mean to be difficult," Virgin said.

Sandy gave her a look. She smiled and he couldn't help laughing.

"Tell me about Garritch," Sandy said.

"I don't like him," Sam said.

"Thanks, Sam, that's helpful."

"Everything you see," Virgin said, "everywhere you go, here, is anchored to the Earth. By people, by life on Earth, by what the Earth is."

"Okay."

"You could say that this is the 'Earthly' Labyrinth. But it isn't limited to that. There's a greater Labyrinth that could extend to the limits of the known Universe and beyond. And there are doors that lead outward."

"Are you saying I could quicken to another planet?"

"If you knew where you were going, theoretically yes. Some have tried, but they've never come back."

Sandy thought about it. "Has anyone come here?"

Sam and Virgin glanced at each other. "It's happened," Sam said.

Sandy waited. "And?"

"I've never met anyone who came through the other way," Sam said. "I've just heard stories."

"What were they?"

"That some were okay, and others …" Sam shrugged.

"Had to be killed," Virgin said.

"She's talking about Itria," Sam said.

"Who's that?"

"Not who, what. An ancient city in the Labyrinth," Virgin said. "There was a visitation by a being from another world. The result was catastrophic. The entire city was laid waste."

"There are *cities* down here?"

"Oh, yeah," Sam said, "a whole lot of them."

"That's what Garritch is worried about," Virgin said. "Things, people, coming here from outside, from other planes of existence. That's why he wants to close all the doors."

"And you don't want that?"

"No," they both said.

"But, if it's dangerous out there, doesn't it make sense to do that?"

"Maybe, if you don't scuttle your ship in the process," Sam said.

"No one knows how many doors there are, Sandy," Virgin said. "Millions, trillions, more—no one knows. Only a small percentage have fixed locations; most of them travel. There's no way to map or predetermine which of them might lead outwards. Garritch has to close all of them to achieve what he's after, and he can't do it one by one. He has to create a cascade, so the doors close on their own. There's no way to know what will happen if he succeeds. There's a danger, a very real danger, that this realm could collapse on itself, maybe even destroy the

Earth. It's possible the collapse could even spread outward, throughout the universe. The doors aren't just passageways, they're connections."

"And he needs Lark—the Quints—to create the cascade."

"He thinks he does," Sam said. "My theory is he's nuts."

"Why does he think he needs her? You said there's stuff I don't know about her. Tell me."

Sam and Virgin glanced at each other.

"The Quints," Virgin said, "is one person, and … *not* one person."

"Please, God," Sandy pleaded, "try not to riddle me this."

Virgin looked off, finding her words, her profile etched against the nameless depths. Sam stood behind her, a character unstuck in place and time, looking the other way. "She's very powerful, Sandy," Virgin said, "in ways I can't explain. Somehow—I don't know how, so don't ask me—she divided herself. She divided her soul into five parts, five people, each responsible for the integrity of one of Five Doors. The doors are special. They *only* provide entrance to or exit from the Earthly labyrinth. If you leave through one of them, you leave the Earth and its Labyrinth behind; if you enter through one, you've come from somewhere else. The doors represent five principles—five attitudes: Love, Acceptance, Appreciation, Respect and Trust. It is with those attitudes that we hope to venture outward, and it is though those doors that we hope to attract seekers from beyond."

"So, you're saying I've only met one part of her."

"Two," Sam said.

"The first you met," Virgin said, "was the Quints of Love. Of that I'm certain. The one at the bar, I don't know. I *think* she was—"

"Appreciation," Sandy, said. He remembered how Lark had embraced him. He stopped walking and stood with his hands on his hips. He'd never felt so made of nameless feelings. "Okay, I need to stop talking about this for awhile." He eyed the Wander. "Where are you taking us?"

The Wander warbled at some length.

"She says she's taking you to someone who can help." Virgin interpreted. "She says she's taking us a long way there to avoid detection."

"Do you believe her?"

Virgin regarded the Wander a moment. "I think so."

Sandy looked at Sam.

He shrugged. "Until I have reason not to."

They trekked on, lapsing into silence. No sense of night or day existed within the cavern. When they grew tired they slept. They stretched out their food as long as they could but eventually their provisions were exhausted, and their water ran out. The Wander warned them not to drink from any of the pools they passed.

Sandy checked the map again and again but it remained entirely blank. No inspiration presented an alternative to following the Wander.

"One of you should take us someplace where we can get food and water," Sandy said, when they stopped again to rest. "We can come back."

The Wander warbled. She had not communicated in a long while.

"She says Garritch would find us," Virgin interpreted.

The Wander warbled again.

"She says it's not much farther," Sam said.

They made themselves move on. Sandy was near to overruling the Wander when the end of the cavern at last came in sight. At the base of the culminating wall four armor-clad sentries bearing long spears guarded the entrance to a passage. Their armor was tinted green and red, a relief from the uniformly yellowish off-white coloration of the cavern.

"Either of you know these guys?" Sandy asked.

Sam and Virgin shook their heads. The Wander told them not to be afraid. That counsel became increasingly difficult to heed as the trio drew near and the size of the sentries became apparent. They stood over ten feet tall.

"They're statues," Virgin said.

Sandy relaxed. They were indeed rendered from stone, their sculptor's art blurred by mineral accretions. The colors in their armor proved to be lichens and moss and minuscule red flowers that bled from crevices in their stone belts and collars and the vents in their helmets.

Above the arched entrance was engraved a symbol composed of hooked lines. As the trio passed between the sentries, the symbol metamorphosed, with a grinding noise, into a pentagram within a circle, and emitted a pale blue glow.

Chapter Fifteen

The Wander led them to a broad, flowstone stairway that descended beyond the scope of sight. The trio stood at the head of the stairs, hesitating, looked back the way they'd come. The Wander warbled and pulsated insistently.

Sandy started down. His companions hastened to flank him. They encountered carvings on the walls, oddly shaped leaves and flowers among sinuous lines suggestive of stylized branches. The deeper they went the denser the carvings became, until they covered the walls in a consuming tangle. The leaves acquired a green tint, the flowers took on blues, reds, yellows and subtler hues. The stairs, too, became green, covered with a thin growth of plant life. The latter thickened, as they continued down, into a cushiony carpet of moss.

The presence of vegetation lightened Sandy's spirits. He gestured at the glowing orb descending ahead of them. "You call this thing a Wander," he said to Virgin. "Why?"

"There are beings in the Labyrinth," she said, "who hold to specific places. I don't know if they are constrained, but they don't travel. Some of them have the

147

ability to project their souls and send them traveling. I've never spoken to anyone who knew why they do that."

"That thing is a soul?"

Virgin smiled. "Comforting, isn't it?"

Sandy glanced at her. "You mean, to know that such a thing exists?"

Her smile broadened.

He thought about it. "Yeah. It is."

The threshold at the foot of the stairs opened onto another cavern, greater, still, than any Sandy had yet encountered, and of a very different character, for it spilled with green life.

Remnants of stone walls rose up through the vegetation; it was evident that there had once been a city here. The plants were like nothing Sandy had seen. Pendulous leaves with blunt, flat ends hung from reed-like branches that rose from the ground in sprays like giant clumps of grass. Giant mushrooms, tree-like, stood thirty or more feet tall, their trunks mossgrown, here and there speckled with tiny purple and scarlet flowers. Giant ferns with variegated fronds rendered the environment jungle-like, arching over the cobblestone path like arbors. Trumpet-shaped flowers, larger than a man's head, opened as Sandy, Virgin and Sam passed, and closed behind them. The diversity of flora was so great a horticulturist might spend a lifetime delineating the taxonomy.

They came upon a mineral pool in which long-legged, spotted crabs dwelt among fat, four-eyed eels and something like two-headed trout. The trio stooped to drink but the Wander whistled and darted to hover over a stream of clear water that ran near the path. The companions knelt on the banks and slaked their thirst.

Sandy heard a rustling noise and peered through a tangle of ferns. He spied a figure in a grey robe bent upon some task. He signaled his companions. "We're not alone," he whispered. Sam and Virgin looked where he pointed.

They backed away quietly and returned to the path, where they found another grey-robed figure, its head turned to look at them. The being was human-like, with arms, legs, torso and head, but it was not human. It had two eyes, in the customary positions on its face, but the lids opened vertically. In place of a nose it had two slits, shaped like inverted tear-drops, and its mouth was a sphincter-like hole.

In its hands it held a bucket and hand trowel, and from its belt hung a claw hand rake and a pair of pruning shears. The creature blinked at them. Seeming to satisfy itself that they posed no threat, it left the path and disappeared into the tangle of flora.

Sam, Virgin and Sandy looked at each other. The Wander whistled and they followed her on down the path. The cavern's ceiling was so distant it might have been sky, though the source of light that illuminated it remained unidentifiable. Light, within the Labyrinth, seemed inherent to place.

A long ways on the vegetation thinned and the path began to climb. They passed out of the jungle and vast terraced gardens opened before them. Tended by scores of grey-robed workers, the gardens ascended to the foot of a majestic palace cut in the cavern's wall. Arrays of windows and patios, interspersed with hanging gardens and exterior walkways, stretched into the distances, right and left. A mammoth flowstone staircase rose to a tall arched entrance.

The Wander shot up the stairs and into the palace, whistling as she went.

Sandy and his companions climbed the stairs, looking around in amazement. The cavern indeed housed the ruins of a great city, translated over the aeons into the cultivated jungle it had become. The latter ended to their left at the shore of a sea so immense its far reaches could not be seen.

The giant stone doors of the palace stood open on a grand hall lined with mineral columns and illumined by fires burning in levitating braziers. Between the columns stone soldiers, like those flanking the entrance in the upper cavern, maintained ceaseless watch.

"I have no knowledge of this place," Virgin said.

"And I have no better option," Sandy said, wagging the map. *A perfect and absolute blank,* he thought. *Fucking Snark hunt.* He folded it and put it back in his pocket. They entered the palace. Going down the hall they passed other broad corridors extending right and left. Sandy pointed at veins of gold striating the walls.

At the hall's far end, another flight of stairs led to another archway. They climbed and entered a high, domed chamber with walls of mottled gold—it gave the impression of having been carved from a gargantuan lode of the element. Veins of a green stone, like serpentine, streaked the walls. A polished stripe of the green stone extended across the floor ahead, like a carpet runner, to another flight of stairs, leading to a high dais. More stone soldiers, these sculpted from the green stone, flanked the path to the dais, atop which a woman robed in regal finery sat upon a massive, green throne.

"Approach," she called, "and be welcome." Her voice, warm and musical, carried with the clarity of a finely wrought instrument. Sam and Sandy did as she bid, but Virgin held back.

"What's wrong?" Sandy asked.

Virgin stood at the threshold, appraising the woman on the throne. She shook her head pensively and joined them.

"Welcome to Morelon," the woman said, when they reached the top of the dais. She had emerald green eyes, elfin features and raven black hair that framed her face in long, wavy tresses. Her robe was a green so dark it was nearly black, embroidered with intricate gold filigree.

"We are Thracia, Queen of this realm." She rose to greet them and her robe fell open, revealing that she was nearly naked underneath. Garments fashioned from a silken, gold material barely covered her breasts and groin. A wave of sexual allure spilled over Sandy so potently that he caught his breath.

Thracia extended her hand, which bore an emerald ring. Virgin and Sam both kissed it, and Sandy copied them. He noticed that the emblem engraved on the ring bore a similarity to one on the coins his grandfather and Gordon had given him: an eye surrounded by a laurel wreath. The wreath on this emblem, though, had thorns.

"We are honored by your gracious welcome, Queen Thracia," said Virgin. "I am Virgin, and this is Sam, anointed archetypes of the Labyrinth. We accompany Alexander, Knight-errant, upon his quest to rescue the Quints, who has been abducted by Garritch Stormcastle, sorcerer most foul and pretender to Wardenship of the Traveling Doors. We were led to you by a Wander."

Thracia smiled at Sandy. "Your quest is known to us," she said. "You serve love and guileless truth. We serve these principles also. You were led to this place by us." Thracia placed her hand on her heart.

Sandy swallowed. The attraction he felt to Thracia rendered him speechless.

Chapter Sixteen

Thracia led them up into her palace. Its structure seemed entirely formed by the arcane guidance of natural forces. Crystals grew in abundance from the walls. Sandy recognized pyrite, hematite, and many forms of quartz. The walls of a reading room they passed were grown entirely with emeralds, and veins of gold ran through the walls everywhere.

The corridors and rooms on the uppermost level were open to the underworld sky, and plant life grew abundantly from the walls, tended, as in the gardens below, by Thracia's legion gardeners.

Thracia led them to a room in which a long, flowstone table had been laid with food.

"Nourish yourselves." The Queen opened her hand at the banquet. "Your battle was arduous, as we know for we witnessed it, and your journey here long and comfortless. Rooms have been prepared for you. After you have eaten, take your rest, and then we will hold council about the ordeals that lie before you."

"Your Highness, if I may ask …"

Thracia left them before Virgin could finish her question.

Sandy and Sam started toward the table but Virgin raised her hand to stop them. She examined the food carefully, smelling each item, tasting, here and there, with the tip of her tongue.

"All right?" Sandy asked.

Virgin twisted her mouth skeptically but nodded. "I think so."

Once they began to eat hunger vanquished caution. None of the fruits and berries were familiar to Sandy, and possessed flavors that were new to him. He found them all delectable. The cooked dishes, composed of fungi and root vegetables, were meaty and satisfying. There was also fermented drink, like wine, that tasted of vanilla and citrus.

When he'd eaten his fill, Sandy sat back, goblet in hand, and gazed upon his companions with fondness. Sam and Virgin sat back, too, and the three smiled at each other and laughed.

"I feel like a weight has been lifted from me," Sandy said.

Virgin looked up at the cavern sky, which had dimmed and acquired a twilight cast, and around at the walls hanging with plants. "It is an oasis of comfort. I wonder about the intentions of our host."

"She's treating us pretty well, isn't she?" Sandy said.

"That doesn't explain why she led us here."

"You think she's got other ideas?" Sam asked.

Virgin continued to look around. "Why greet us like that? On her throne. Why all the pomp?"

"She's a Queen," Sandy said.

"Yes, very theatrical with the *pluralis majestatis.* Where are her subjects? All I see are these gardeners."

"How many subjects do you need to be a Queen? Maybe she doesn't get to show off much."

"*You* liked her, I noticed," Virgin said.

Sandy made a face. "Well, I'm not *dead.*"

Virgin and Sam laughed.

"She led me to the Archetype's bar. She helped us fight Garritch. She hasn't given us any reason to doubt her—" Sandy hoisted the pitcher—"and this is some pretty good stuff."

"Won't argue that." Sam held out his goblet for Sandy to refill.

"Have you ever eaten such food?" Sandy asked.

"Some of the fruits I'm familiar with," Virgin said. "They only grow in the Labyrinth."

"I've come across a couple of them in Keel." Sam pointed at a blue, kumquat-like fruit, and a bowl of green, bean-shaped berries.

"Keel?" Sandy asked.

"A city in the Labyrinth."

Sandy shook his head. "I'm never going to understand this place, am I?"

"People spend their lives trying to unlock its mysteries," Virgin said. "Long study changes them. You've met one."

"Seems like I've met a bunch."

"One in particular."

Sandy met her gaze. "The Hierophant."

She nodded.

"So, everyone down here is an archetype?"

"No." Sam shook his head.

"Very few of the inhabitants of the Labyrinth are archetypes," Virgin said. "Less than one percent. Much less."

"How do you know you are one? Because you can go to the bar?"

"Oh, no," Sam said, "a lot of archetypes never go there."

"How then?"

"It's mostly your appearance, not being able to control it. Your clothes, sometimes."

"Or lack thereof," said Virgin.

"You can't change clothes?"

"When I'm alone I can wear what I want," Sam said. "I walk out the door and, foop! it's back to this." He pointed at his hat.

"For me it's different," Virgin said. "When I'm with small groups of friends, I can wear what I want. I always put clothes on, but when I'm around large groups, foop! as Sam says, back to the clamshell."

"On Earth, too?"

"Only in the Labyrinth."

"Do people give you trouble?"

"If they do they learn not to."

"I imagine a medieval halberd is a helpful teaching aid."

"It can be."

"Was Virgin always your name?"

"No, I just figured out what I personified and quit fighting it. My birth name was Beatrice Cloutier."

"I used to be William Braden," Sam said. "Down here I got tired of 'Bogie' so I went with 'Sam.'"

"Has it affected you in … other ways?"

"Like what?" Sam asked.

Sandy swirled the wine in his goblet. "Before I came here I was forty-two—" he downed the wine—"and not nearly so fit." He smacked his lips.

Virgin chuckled softly. "I was eighty-seven when I left the order."

Sandy stared at her. "Holy shit." He looked at Sam. "You?"

"I'm as I was. Didn't change at all, except for the restricted wardrobe, and haven't changed since. The Labyrinth affects people differently."

Sandy started to pour himself more wine and stopped. "Lark is an archetype, isn't she?"

"More than one, I think," Sam said.

"Five?"

"I don't know about that."

"How old is *she?*"

Virgin looked at Sam.

"Tell him," Sam said. "He should know."

"The Labyrinth extends life," Virgin said, "beyond anything you could hope for on Earth. For some it extends it more than others."

"Is she older than you?" Sandy asked.

Virgin sighed and nodded. "Considerably. I don't know exactly how old, but, as time is measured on Earth, hundreds of years at least."

Sandy set down his goblet. "You've got to be kidding me."

Sam and Virgin were silent.

Sandy slumped back in his chair. "What have I gotten into?"

"Would you have done it differently, if you'd known?" Sam asked.

Sandy remembered his safe, predictable life. "I don't know."

"Look at me," Sam said.

Sandy was startled by the intensity of Sam's gaze.

"Not long ago you would have clocked me if I'd questioned your feelings for that woman. Has that changed?"

Sandy remembered Lark kneeling beside him, laughing, with the stars in her hair. "No."

Sam nodded. "You're here. Now. That didn't happen by accident, and nobody tricked you. You've found out the way you used to figure things doesn't work anymore. You tell me, did it ever?"

Sandy remembered how losing Lark had confronted him with the voids in his life. "No, it did not."

"Right. People get old, Sandy, and they die. That's a fact of flesh. It doesn't change who they are. *That's* the illusion."

"But time does change people, Sam," Sandy said. "Hundreds of years—" he looked at Virgin—"maybe more?" He shook his head. "How can I measure up to that?"

"She wouldn't have picked you—"

"She *didn't* pick me."

"She would not have *accepted* you," Virgin said, "if you couldn't. She would not have *recognized* you."

Silence dragged between them. Sam cleared his throat, poured Sandy more wine and lifted his own goblet. "To love."

The defiance in Sam's attitude reached Sandy. Yes, one moment in his life stood out from all the rest. He raised his goblet and Virgin raised hers.

"Here's looking at you, kid." Sam winked at Virgin.

The sky continued to darken. Candles and braziers throughout the chamber came alight. Three of the grey-robed attendants entered the hall. In a high, whistling voice, one of them said, "We will lead you to your quarters."

Sandy and his companions, ready enough for rest, followed the Queen's servants out of the banquet hall and down a flight of stairs into a long corridor.

One of the attendants stopped at a door and, nodding at Virgin, extended its hand.

Sam was reluctant to leave her.

She stroked his cheek affectionately. "We should not distract ourselves this night, I think."

He kissed her hand. Sandy and he followed the two remaining attendants on down the corridor.

"*Are* these her only subjects, you think?" Sandy asked quietly.

"Who knows," Sam said. "I'm not sure she's human. I don't think she ever leaves this place."

"You think Virgin's right to be worried?"

"I think it would be unwise to get too comfortable."

An enormous archway, on the left side of the passage, opened onto an immense, dark chamber. Sandy saw something inside and paused to look.

Sam stepped back to look with him. "What is that?"

Sandy frowned. "A big skeleton. Looks like a dinosaur."

"Your rooms are this way," the attendants said.

Sam and Sandy followed them.

One of the attendants stopped at another open door, and gestured to Sam. Sam paused at the threshold. "I never ignore what Virgin says."

Sandy followed the remaining attendant. It led him on a ways and turned left into a short corridor, at the end of which was a single door. The attendant opened the door and extended its hand.

The room was strange in many ways, but sumptuous in its comforts. Shelf fungi of many colors grew from the walls, and the chairs and divans, formed of flowstone, were grown with thick cushions of moss. The canopy bed was more conventional in its makeup, bearing fine linen sheets, and thick, white pillows. The bedspread was woven with foliar patterns.

The servant indicated a basin, into which water ran from a spout, and a round, flowstone-rimmed pool full of steaming water.

"Do you require assistance with your bath?" the attendant asked.

Sandy shot the creature an incredulous look. "I'll manage, thank you."

The attendant bowed and withdrew.

Sandy took off his jacket and for the first time studied the woven emblem on its breast. It was shield-shaped, like a heraldic coat of arms, with a white peony sinister chief and five columns dexter chief on a green background above a red chevron. He touched it, becoming quiet inside, and folded the jacket over a chair.

By the basin were a pearl-handled straight razor, a wooden comb, and a wood-handled toothbrush. There was also a vial of green, soapy fluid, and by the toothbrush a dish of white powder. Sandy shaved with care and brushed his teeth, undressed and sank with a sigh into the warm, mineral pool. The wound at the base of his ear itched. He peeled off Appox's bandage and felt the stitches. The wound was healing. He left the bandage off. Tension eased from his muscles, and he lay in the pool awhile, letting his thoughts and baffling memories of the last few days jumble through his mind without trying to make sense of them.

He forced himself to get out before he fell asleep. The towels the servant left him had the feel of warm grass, but were absorbent and pleasant against his skin. He climbed into bed naked. The sheets, mattress and pillows were soft and welcoming. The lights in the room dimmed and went out. Sandy pulled up the covers and fell soon asleep.

CHAPTER SEVENTEEN

He dreamed that he stood before a wooden door in an old stone wall, in the company of a young boy. The boy smiled a disarming smile and gestured at the door.

Sandy pushed the door open to behold a verdant land of rolling hills, above which kite-like creatures swooped through the air in a random aerial ballet. The boy led Alexander along a cobbled path to a staircase that rose into the sky.

The boy climbed the stairs, beckoning Sandy to follow. Sandy climbed after him, and soon, in the manner of dreams, they were high above the land, among the clouds, where the staircase ended at another door.

The boy went through the doorway, and again Sandy followed. He found himself on a dais among the stars. At the opposite side of the dais were five thrones, situated before five archways that framed views of the encompassing firmament.

Three of the thrones were occupied by women whom Sandy immediately recognized to be Lark. One had red hair, as Lark had when Sandy first encountered her, another the auburn tresses she'd had in *Le Cabaret d'Archétypes*. The third had blond hair braided like a crown. All three sat with their eyes closed and seemed unaware of his presence.

Sandy was joyous to see Lark. He understood the three versions before him to be reflections of a single person. He tried to speak to her but had no voice.

"You can't reach her that way," the boy said, with a mischievous smile.

Something about him was familiar.

"Don't you know me, old friend?" the boy said.

Sandy realized the boy was Gordon. "You're a child again!" Sandy exclaimed, finding his voice.

Gordon shook his head. "Honoring our first meeting."

"What?"

"It was *you* who visited my childhood dream, Sandy. You introduced me to the Labyrinth."

"Gordon, I hadn't even been born."

"Our friendship extends beyond this life." Gordon became serious. "You have to wake up, now, Alexander."

Sandy shook his head. He didn't want to wake up.

"I said *wake up!*" Gordon screamed.

Sandy sat up, aware of another presence in the room, heard a faint rustling like someone hurrying away stealthily. He swung his legs out of bed and the braziers came alight. His jacket lay on the floor.

He checked the pockets. His wallet, coin and map were there, but the vernier caliper was gone.

Sandy pulled on his clothes. The candles lining the hallway outside did not come alight when he stepped out of his room. He went back and took the candlestick from his bedside.

He tried to remember where Sam and Virgin's rooms were. At the end of the short hall that led to his room, he couldn't remember whether to turn right or left.

The chamber where he'd seen the giant skeleton—that had been to the right, he felt certain. Sam had been with him when he'd looked in there.

He tried the doors as he went. Most were locked. He opened one that wasn't and called out, but received no answer. The chamber was overgrown with moss and fungus, no evidence of furnishings anywhere.

He pressed on, reached the broad archway where he'd seen the giant skeleton and knew he'd gone too far. An urge stronger than curiosity drew him to explore the chamber.

The skeleton resembled a dinosaur in size, but the skull didn't belong to any creature Sandy knew. He held the candle high and saw long bones arching above him. Extending from massive humeri that articulated with the skeleton's shoulder blades, they fanned, finger-like to the limits of the room.

Wings. Giant wings.

"My God," he whispered.

"He was a God," said a voice behind him.

Levitating braziers came alight around the chamber's circumference as Thracia entered. She was not wearing her robe. Sandy turned his attention to the gargantuan skeleton and saw it whole. It should have long since collapsed in a heap, but some agency held it intact.

"It's a dragon, isn't it?"

"That is only a word," Thracia said. "His name was Melchior. He once ruled a great expanse of the Labyrinth. He was known in the Earthly realm as well, in ancient times. His power was beyond restriction." Her voice became wistful. "Unlike mine." She walked to the skull and stroked it sadly. "He was a great friend."

"How did he die?"

"He tired of living. He was very old. One night he came here, went to sleep and never awakened."

Sandy felt Thracia's loneliness. It roused his desire to give comfort, but he remembered why he woke up. "You took my caliper."

"It will be returned to you. I do not allow weapons within the palace."

"You could have said so."

Thracia stepped close. "My servants are meek and gentle. It is not in them to make demands. They follow my instructions as unobtrusively as they can." She stroked Sandy's face. His skin flared with elation. Her body radiated narcotic warmth. "Do not be angry with me, Knight-errant. I rarely have visitors, and become forgetful of my manners. You are right, I should have told you. Accept my apology."

Sandy was beyond feeling anything for Thracia but pity and desire. He strove to remain nonchalant. "Of course." He saw how very alone she was. "You can't leave this place?"

"Not without great cost, a cost to which I am unwilling to accede." She gazed about reflectively. "Morelon is much diminished from what it was in Melchior's time." She smiled at Sandy. "But it is my home. Some day, if one who is Melchior's equal relieves me of my place upon the throne, I may roam free. But that time is not come." She took Sandy's arm. He thrilled, again, at her touch. Her scent was a garden. "Are you still tired? Do you wish to return to your bed?"

He swallowed. "I'm awake."

"Join me, then. Keep me company."

Thracia led Sandy back into the corridor, and upstairs to her chambers. Along the way they spoke of trivial matters, and he made her laugh, and all thought of Lark left his mind.

Chapter Eighteen

Thracia's bedroom was a citadel unto itself, its domed roof open at its center to the cavern sky. Levitating braziers and candles illuminated a space greater than her throne room. The plants and fungi that grew from the walls reached to her as she passed. At its far end, a great archway opened onto a broad terrace and the cavern beyond. Luminescent plants in the gardens and jungle rendered the expanse of Morelon perceptible in the darkness. The ocean, too, extending to unknown shores, gave off a pale light of its own.

Thracia led Sandy to an unfurnished space in the floor, perhaps fifty feet square, with pillows at one end. He did not resist when she undressed him, and she shed the minute garments she wore. She stepped onto the open space. Its surface gave beneath her feet, and Sandy saw it was the sunken mattress of a giant bed. She drew back the covers and beckoned him. He joined her and they lay down together. Thracia took him into her arms, and he was lost in the ocean of her, overcome with rapturous delight. She caressed his genitals, not letting him enter her, took him repeatedly to the brink of release.

"Stay with me," she whispered. "Rule Morelon at my side. Together we can restore its glory. Renounce your quest, Alexander. Remain with me as my mate and equal, and be a father to my children."

Sandy groaned in assent, ready to agree to anything to consummate his passion.

"Say the words, my love. Tell me that you forsake your quest, and by your own will choose to stay with me."

He opened his mouth to do as she bid, but a tiny voice in his mind stopped him. *Think,* it said; *think before you speak.*

He didn't want to think, but the voice grew more insistent. Sandy became aware of a cloud in his mind, amid the tides and flurries of ecstasy. Lark's face emerged. *Come to me, Alexander,* she said; *come to me and be free.*

Sandy opened his eyes. Thracia held his gaze, her eyes mesmerizing and beseeching. He forced himself to think about what she was asking of him, saw how close he had come to betraying Lark, and shame poured through him, blighting sensual joy. He did not want to let go of the joy. The will to do so was beyond him—infinitely easier to yield to transcendence of time and cares.

Somewhere a distant bang sounded, followed by several others. Shouts and sounds of conflict, footsteps running near ...

Sandy pulled a little away from Thracia, less than an inch, and saw in her eyes what he had not before: cunning. The ecstasy of immersion dissolved in loss.

Sam and Virgin burst into Thracia's chambers. Virgin guarded the door and Sam ran to the bedside, his revolver aimed at Thracia.

"Put your clothes on," he told Sandy. "She's cast a pall on your mind."

Thracia drew up on her bed. Her eyes turned molten, red flames licking from their orbits. "How *dare* you violate my chambers!" she roared, her rumbling voice octaves deeper than it had been.

Sam advanced on her, gun aimed at her heart. "You know the nature of my weapon. You are not immune to it."

Sandy dragged himself from the bed. His erection throbbed painfully. Sam helped him stand, keeping his revolver trained on Thracia.

"Pull it together, pal. We need to scram."

Thracia was changing, her face elongating, her body and limbs swelling and lengthening. Her skin darkened and became scaly.

Sandy forced himself to pull on his clothes. "She took—" he gasped for breath—"she took my talisman."

Sam reached in his coat and held Sandy's vernier caliper out to him. The instant Sandy had it, power surged through him and the caliper unfolded into a sword.

Thracia became gigantic. Wings grew from her shoulders, and a tail from the base of her spine. Sandy understood, then, what she was, and the nature of her confinement. He ran across the room behind Sam, but stopped at the door. Thracia was fully transformed. Sandy looked with compassion into her baleful dragon eyes, and for an instant saw them soften with regret.

"I'm sorry," he said, and ran out. "Do you know how to go?" he called after Sam.

"I do!" Virgin answered, far ahead. "But look at your map!"

Sandy pulled out the map and shook it open. "Nothing!"

"Talk to it!" Virgin yelled. "Command it! She's been interfering with it!"

Sandy had difficulty holding the map open with one hand while running. He shook the sword in frustration. "Change into a fucking caliper!" he shouted. The sword collapsed into a vernier caliper shaped like a penis. Sandy goggled. "I mean … what you were when I got you!" It reshaped into its original form. He put it in his pocket and held the map open with both hands. "Show me!" he ordered.

An ember came alight at the center of the map and spread in a smoldering ring that expanded across the paper, burning away the enchantment that had concealed its true surface. The underlying map showed an aerial diagram of Morelon. Words at the top read: *Morelon, Itria of Old.*

"Aw, *shit!*" Sandy cried.

"What is it?" Sam asked.

"You don't want to know. We *need* to get out of here."

"Are we going the right way?" Virgin called.

Sandy studied the map. It changed and showed a diagram of the interior of the palace, with three arrows traveling down a corridor. The arrows had to be him and his companions; a dotted line extended in front of them. "There should be a stairway coming up on the right."

Virgin led them down a broad switchback of stairs, then left, through a corridor to the entrance hall. The stone guards were coming to life, cracking and shedding stone, exposing genuine armor beneath. Their eyes lighted with fire.

"Come on!" Sam shouted.

They raced down the aisle between the animated soldiers. Some of the soldiers groped for them. Their movements were sluggish, but becoming less so. Five grouped together, swords drawn, blocking the entrance.

"Hit 'em with all you got!" Sam shouted. He fired at the guards. Two went down and broke apart. Others moved to replace them.

Sandy shoved the map in his pocket and drew his caliper, opening both sword and armor. Virgin, clad in chain mail, had her halberd. The trio engaged with the guards blocking the entrance. Sam dodged between them and ducked under their legs, fanning his pistol. Virgin stabbed, hacked and battered in a lethal dance. Sandy thrust and swung his sword, cutting an arm from one soldier and stabbing another through the chest.

They broke through and ran down the stairs, into the Labyrinthine night of Morelon. At the bottom Sandy commanded his sword to become a caliper again and pulled out the map, which gave off its own light, now. The traveling arrows pointed toward the sea. "This way!" he shouted.

They ran diagonally down across the terraced gardens and into the jungle, fragments of luminescent plant life clinging to their skin and clothing. The glowing vegetation came alive, grabbing and pulling at them. Sandy took the lead and hacked a way through. A thunder of boots sounded to their left.

"They're flanking us," Sam said.

Sandy redoubled his efforts, slashing through writhing ferns. He could see the water ahead. What they would do when they reached the shore he didn't know.

A shadow passed overhead and they were briefly blinded as the jungle before them burst into flames. Thracia swung wide through the air to come at them again. They dodged left around the burning vegetation and the soldiers double-timed toward them.

When Thracia flew close again, Sam shot her in the wing. She dodged away and dove, shrieking in pain. They reached the edge of the jungle and won the shore, but the soldiers were nearly on them.

"Run, Sandy!" Virgin said. "We'll hold them!"

"I'm not leaving you!"

She backhanded him across the face. "Do not die here for nothing! Run! Finish your quest!"

He stumbled backward, watching his friends fight for him. Two soldiers broke past them and he cut them down.

"Run!" Virgin yelled.

He turned and ran down the beach, around the shoulder of the palace. He collapsed his sword and armor and pulled out the map. The arrow pointed ahead, past the palace, where the shoreline paralleled the wall of the cavern. The luminescent ocean swept out to his left.

Sandy settled into a loping run, sounds of battle dwindling behind him. He did not know how Sam and Virgin could stand down such a force, or how he would manage without them. He felt a coward, leaving them behind.

The farther he ran the more convinced he became that his friends had died. He kept expecting Thracia to descend on him. She never did, and he supposed Sam must have wounded her badly. Every time Sandy reached a threshold of exhaustion he thought of Sam and Virgin and pushed through it, vowing that their sacrifice would not be in vain. He tethered himself to Lark's image in his mind.

He did not know how long he ran. The sound of the surf drew him into a hypnagogic state, and he slapped himself to stay awake. He encountered a stone outcrop that jutted into the water from the cavern wall, and fell against it, trembling and panting.

He found a narrow hole in the outcrop, squirmed through it, and dropped to the shore on the other side. He patted the rocks, glad to have a barrier between himself and pursuers. A few steps on his legs failed, and he collapsed unconscious to the sand.

CHAPTER NINETEEN

Alexander awoke to the sound of lapping surf. It was light out again. His mouth was dry as ashes.

He pushed himself up, and sat with his eyes closed, breathing. Every part of him ached.

He sensed that he was not alone, blinked his eyes open.

A woman in a white robe knelt before him, blindfolded, with her back to the sea. She held two swords with the blades crossed over her head.

"Alexander," she said, in a quiet, clear voice.

Sandy struggled to his feet. "Lark." He staggered toward her.

"Yes, I am here."

Sandy knew he was not addressing the Quints of Love, but another. Still, it *was* her, and warmth filled his heart in her presence.

"I feel your love," she said, her voice quavering.

"Why are you blindfolded? Why do you come to me like this?"

"Garritch knows the connection between us. He fears you, Alexander, but you are not ready to face him. If I look upon you, he will see you through my eyes, and know you are here."

"Tell me what to do."

"He has sent a Behemoth after me, a terrible creature that prowls the Labyrinthine seas. It will find me—it is inescapable. Even now it approaches."

"Then let's get you away from the water." He reached to help her stand.

"No," she said. "We cannot escape the Behemoth in this place. Even if we could it would not matter. So long as any of my aspects are bound, the rest are fated to fall under Garritch's sway."

Sandy swallowed. "And he already has two."

"Three," she said, "at the time that we found each other, Garritch had already seized one of my aspects."

"So, you *were* looking for me."

"No, only looking. I gave myself to the will of the Labyrinth and it led me to you. It led us to each other."

"But you knew what would happen to me."

Lark's head drooped. "Do you regret finding me?"

Sandy knelt before her. "No, my love, I do not."

She smiled faintly, with sadness. "Garritch holds my captive aspects apart, and confuses their minds so we cannot join. I came here to beseech you, Alexander—it is a terrible thing that no one should ever be asked to do—but please, if you *are* willing, do what the Hierophant counseled. Cross the Endless Plain. There are barriers in your mind that prevent you from knowing your strength. The ordeal is horrific; we are desperate or I would not ask it of you. You have to relinquish your identity to unmask your inner self. Only then will you be able to find the Citadel of the Maimed, and free my aspects."

Sandy cupped Lark's face in his hand. "I'm not going to let him take you."

"No, Alexander, you cannot defend me here. I came only to urge you to fulfill your quest." She turned her head toward the sea. "The beast comes. I cannot quicken you from this place; Garritch has closed the doors around me. Flee, Alexander. You must not be taken."

Sandy helped Lark to her feet. "I'm not going to leave you."

She started to object further but again turned her head and was overcome by a dismal perception. Her mouth twisted with self rebuke. "I should not have come here. I have failed you, and put you in danger. I have failed everyone."

"No, no, don't think that."

She shook her head. "This is what Garritch wanted. Always he seeks to pervert me. I have been stupid and selfish, and endangered everyone."

"Don't talk that way about the woman I love."

"I should have trusted you," she said, sobbing.

"Trust me now."

Lark fell against him and he held her. She calmed herself, took a deep breath, straightened and set her chin. "The Behemoth is invisible. You cannot see this creature with your eyes, Alexander, only with your mind. Close your eyes and visualize the sea."

Sandy took out his caliper and shook it into a sword. He faced the ocean at Lark's side, captured the image of the sea in his mind and closed his eyes.

He held the image inwardly. It wavered, jostled by concerns, then steadied into focus. The waves rolled in and all seemed quiescent. Sandy could see Lark, too, in his mind, her blindfold gone.

She looked him up and down with uncertainty. "The most we can hope to achieve is your escape," she said. "You cannot save me."

We'll see about that.

The lapping of the water became irregular. With a sound like a burst of steam, a grey, fleshy dome, covered with knurled creases, rose from the sea. The water sluiced from its surface and the creases parted, revealing hundreds of eyes.

The dome rose until it loomed mammoth above them. A geyser spewed from a blowhole in its crown. The water around its base swarmed with movement, and glassy, translucent tendrils—thousands, maybe millions of them—snaked across the beach towards Lark and Sandy.

"It only wants to capture *me*, Alexander. You it will kill."

Sandy gripped the handle of his sword more tightly, and his armor unfolded. Seeing the full nature of the monster, he knew that Lark had been right. He could not defeat it. The Behemoth's tendrils squirmed on the sand, whipped out and grabbed them.

Sandy and Lark fought together, cutting themselves free only to be seized again and again. Tendrils grabbed Sandy's blade and sword arm, and he nearly lost his weapon, but Lark slashed him free. She became enshrouded with tendrils and he hacked them off of her. The behemoth bellowed in pain through its blowhole, but continued its attack. It advanced onto the beach and overwhelmed them.

Tendrils tightened around Sandy, crushing his armor to his flesh. He roared in rage and agony.

Sandy heard an answering roar and felt a blast of heat. The tendrils loosened their hold, let go and withdrew. He fell from their grasp. Above him a dragon flapped in the air, breathing fire at the Behemoth. The monster retreated into the water in a thrashing churn.

Thracia settled onto the beach by Lark and Sandy. They both could hardly move. Sandy forced himself to his knees, fearing Thracia might seize him and bear him back to her palace to make him her plaything. But the dragon hung her head, coughing smoke. She diminished, her wings, claws and tail retracting, resumed her human form, and collapsed naked on the beach. In her right shoulder was a bloody wound.

Sandy retracted his armor and blade. He put the vernier caliper back in his pocket and leaned on his knees, watching Thracia.

"Thank you," he said.

"It will return." She winced, gripping her wounded shoulder. "I cannot fight it again. I am beyond the limit of my domain. My powers are spent."

As if in answer to her words, a geyser erupted from the water. Thracia gestured at it in resignation. Sandy closed his eyes and saw the Behemoth again rise from the sea.

Many of the beast's eyes were squeezed shut. Its skin was blistered where Thracia had burned it. It sent its tendrils out more cautiously, now, encircling Thracia, Sandy and Lark, all three. The tendrils mounded up in a squirming mass, slowly encroaching.

Lark thrust her swords in the sand, climbed to her feet and tore off her blindfold. She helped Sandy up and held his face. He nearly wept to see how red and bloodied she was from the Behemoth's assault. Her eyes cleared with recognition.

"I wanted to hear your voice before he took me," she said.

She kissed him and he took her in his arms. His being filled with courage and strength.

"I trust you, my love," she said. "Come find me." She pulled her swords from the sand and faced the beast with her eyes closed. Sandy saw what she intended and started after her, but Thracia restrained him.

Lark charged the Behemoth and leapt upon its towering dome with a fierce cry. She stabbed two of its eyes and the beast howled in pain through its blowhole. It withdrew its tendrils from around Thracia and Sandy, wrapped them around Lark and sank back into the sea. There was a sudden slump in the water that settled and calmed.

Thracia loosened her hold and Sandy shook her off. He charged into the water but there was nothing to fight but waves. He sank to his knees in the surf and wept.

"She took it through the only door left open to her," Thracia said, "to Garritch's stronghold, wherever that is. It won't come back, now."

"Why did you *stop* me?"

"Don't be ridiculous." Thracia groaned tiredly. "I have to return to Morelon."

"You mean *Itria*," he spat.

She didn't respond. Sandy slogged back onto the beach. Thracia averted her eyes.

"It was an accident," she said, and sank onto a rock. "We came through the wrong way. We only wanted to cross over. They thought we meant harm and we had to defend ourselves." She studied the cavern's inscrutable heights. Waves lapped at the shoreline. "Shame robbed Melchior of his will to live." She looked at Sandy. "*Shame.*"

"Over the destruction of the city?"

She stared down the beach without answering.

Sandy didn't want to know about anyone else's pain. He had enough of his own.

"I was pregnant," Thracia said finally. She stood up, holding her shoulder. "My children have been trapped in a nascent state for millennia, paying for our mistake. We're not like you. Our offspring can't be human or dragon, either one, without a father."

The quiet lapping of the surf filled the silence between them. "My friends?" Sandy asked.

"They live. I will release them." Thracia seemed slight and frail against the monolithic backdrop of the cavern wall.

"Why me?" Sandy asked. "I'm no one special."

Thracia mustered a wan smile. "You do not know yourself."

People kept telling him that. "I'm sorry we killed so many of your soldiers."

"They are animations. You killed no one."

"I couldn't stay with you."

"I know." She gazed down the beach, again. "Finish your quest, Alexander. You are worthy of her, and she of you." Thracia reached down and picked up a flask from behind the rock she'd sat on, tossed it to Sandy. "I thought you might be thirsty."

Sandy brushed sand from the flask. "I'm not a dragon, Thracia."

She gave him a wry grin. "Not yet."

Sandy watched the Queen of Morelon climb through the hole in the stone outcrop, and he was alone again.

CHAPTER TWENTY

Sandy drained the flask, then wished he hadn't. He didn't know how long it would be before he'd find drinkable water again and he was still thirsty.

He didn't want to linger where the Behemoth had come ashore. The map represented the wall on his right as a jagged line, the waters to his left, identified as *The Sea of Nomenclature,* as a few wavy lines in a region without a far boundary. The area beyond the cavern wall bore no referent whatsoever.

Sandy regarded the blank space dully. "'The Great Void of Whatever, I guess," he muttered. His words appeared on the map, in the unmarked region, just as he'd spoken them: *The Great Void of Whatever I Guess.*

He narrowed his gaze at the map and its persistent arrow. "You're a barrel of laughs." He folded it and put it back in his pocket, trudged on down the beach, hoping Thracia was good as her word, and Sam and Virgin would be allowed to rejoin him. He didn't want to be alone with his thoughts. He kept seeing Lark in the grip of the Behemoth.

Everyone seemed to think he had powers, but the strength that came to him when he gripped his sword mystified him. The man who wielded the sword in battle was a stranger. He bore no resemblance to any person Sandy had understood himself to be throughout his earlier life.

However much confidence others placed in him, he remained unconvinced of his capacity to contend with the forces aligned against him; yet here he was, marching forth to contend with them. He didn't know where he was or where he was going, and had nothing but an enigmatic arrow to guide him.

It struck him that a similar predicament confronted one at birth, arriving in the world ignorant of where or why, assembling answers by happenstance. He remembered Sam's response when he'd asked him about the location of the Labyrinth. Names, conferred and handed down, veiled the intractable mysteries of both place and identity.

He remembered discussing matters of deportment with friends as a child—how to wipe one's ass, what to think about girls and how much to engage with them, the thrill of forbidden words. It all seemed cut from whole cloth, arbitrary and circumstantial.

Sandy saw himself from a distance, in his mind, a minuscule, insubstantial entity in a fathomless cosmos, set on a course he had accepted blindly. He had no answer to his doubts, but he knew he was guided by more than a blinking arrow.

He was guided by love. Foolishly, perhaps, but the finding of another, the surrendering to a truth in closeness that reached the pith of the soul, that beauty, that opening, what was life without that? If he had to pick among incomprehensible motives with which to decide the course of his life, he would choose it above all others.

He did not need to understand.

His map rustled in his pocket. He frowned, pulled it out and it snapped open in his hands. The arrow had changed direction. It seemed to be telling him to leave the beach and take a diagonal course into the water.

There was another mark on the map that hadn't been there before, a bold 'x' marking something on the beach ahead. Diving into the sea for no reason didn't make sense, and Sandy wasn't sure he trusted Thracia about the Behemoth not coming back. He wanted to see what the 'x' was about.

He tried to fold the map back up but it kept reopening, every time he tried to put it in his jacket. He wadded it up and shoved it in his pants, headed for the 'x.' Around a bend in the cavern wall he found Garritch in his long coat, waiting for him.

Sandy strode toward him. Any concern about his capacity for violence withered in the heat of his wrath.

He stopped a few paces from Garritch and the two regarded each other.

"Alexander Creaze," Garritch said.

"Scumbag."

"You stand against me."

Sandy shook his head. "I stand for Lark."

Garritch grinned. "Which one?"

"There's only one."

"And I have her."

"Not yet you don't."

Garritch glanced up and gestured at the sky. "Do you know what's up there?"

Sandy didn't respond.

"Nor do I. Nor does anyone. Stars, space, what this place becomes outside of our domain—no one knows. But we want to go there. Some of us do. Without any fore-knowledge of the horrors we might call back on ourselves. That doesn't seem foolhardy to you? I'd think we'd do better to look after what we've got."

"I don't really know much about it."

"That would be exactly my point."

"No one knows how their lives will turn out. I've spent long enough playing it safe."

"And you'd make that decision for everyone."

"No, but you would, apparently."

"'Love, Appreciation, Acceptance, Trust, Respect—' those are postures, not perspectives."

"Just you say so."

"You're on the wrong side, Mister Creaze."

Sandy remembered the grey-haired stranger in the Archetype's Club. "You think there are sides?"

"You're with me or you're against me."

"Those are my only options, eh?"

"They are."

"We'll see. Here's where I stand. You're holding the woman I love against her will, and trying to use her for your purposes. Over my dead fucking body, clear enough?"

"And if you unite all of her aspects, and it turns out she does not want you, what then?"

"That would be her choice. Not mine and not yours."

"How gallant. You expect me to believe you pursue your quest with no hope for yourself?"

"I have hopes. They don't include making her decisions for her."

"But you would let her make my decisions for me."

"Like I said, I don't know much about this argument. I do know that opening a door is not the same as making anyone walk through it. Closing a door, on the other hand, imposes a restriction. Closing all doors is a lot of restriction."

"Not close them forever. Close them and open them selectively. Judiciously. Prudently."

"Yeah, that sounds good, except *you* wind up holding all the keys. If I *liked* you I'd have a problem with that."

"And you don't like me."

"Not even a little."

Garritch peered off, with a supercilious smile. The symbols glimmering in his coat were in a constant state of flux. "Why am I bothering with you? You're powerless against me. You're not even smart enough to know it."

Sandy pulled out his caliper and willed it into a sword.

Garritch laughed. He thrust his right hand into the air, clenched it and was gone.

Sandy collapsed his sword and put it back in his pocket. The beach extended indefinitely before him, empty of answers. His aggressions had accomplished nothing. He'd chased bad men, and they'd run from him—scant joy for they'd gotten away. He'd survived battles but felt no sense of victory.

He decided he might as well wait where he was for Sam and Virgin, and faced the sea. He noticed a rise in the water, out a ways, and wondered what manner of leviathan might cause such a swell in this bizarre realm, hoping it wasn't the Behemoth. The rise acquired a frothy crest and Sandy realized it was a massive wave, headed towards him.

There was no time to run, nowhere to run to. All he could do was watch. In the moment before it took him, Sandy remembered Garritch's parting gesture, and knew the sorcerer had caused this.

Like a giant maw, the wave swallowed him, and Sandy was churned about like a morsel. He tried desperately to swim to the surface. But light was all of a kind, around him, with no direction of greater brightness.

Luminous things swirled with him. One that was fish-like swam close. It proved to be a glowing word in the shape of a fish. '*Perch*,' it read, and another, nearby, read '*trout*.'

Other words, in many languages, became perceptible in the myriad swirl. In English he read '*I-beam*,' '*anorak*,' '*chicken*,' '*pipe wrench*,' '*cauliflower*,' and '*dodecahedron*,' all spelled in the shapes of the things they named.

He spotted one that read '*door*.' On instinct he swam toward it. The word, like an elusive rhyme, tossed away from him. Sandy strove after it, the air in his lungs souring, the demand to inhale aching in his chest.

It seemed he wouldn't make it, and a misery of despair swept through him, that he would fail Lark in this way. *Come to me*, he thought desperately, watching '*door*' sink into distance. He was about to give up when the word, borne by a random current, lilted back in his direction. Sandy pushed with his remaining strength, reached the word and, not knowing what else to do, swam through it.

He was deposited, coughing and gasping, in a dim chamber of rough-hewn stone. He pushed himself up on hands and knees, catching his breath, surprised to be alive.

He stood and took in his surroundings. The chamber seemed a kind of alcove, giving onto a larger space a few feet ahead. Looking back, Sandy saw a wavering rectangle lose coherence and vanish. It came to him what the map had tried to show him. He pulled it from his pants pocket and carefully smoothed it out.

The map dried swiftly in his hands. It showed the alcove and the greater chamber beyond. At the far limit of the latter, a break in the linear boundary bore the word, *'Exit.'* The space beyond lacked any feature except the words, *'Endless Plain.'*

Sandy heartened to see those words. That was exactly where he wanted to go. But then he saw other marks encroaching around the periphery of the outer chamber— a proliferation of x's.

Sandy pocketed the map and ventured out, drawing his sword. Creatures malformed and menacing, some man-like, some composed of less recognizable flesh, with tentacles and pincers for limbs, emerged from cracks in the walls. They crowded the chamber in a great horde, blocking Sandy's way.

PART THREE

THE DESERT OF LANGUOROUS TORMENTS

CHAPTER TWENTY-ONE

The patrons of the Dire Disputes Saloon had been tolerating each other a long while. Most busied themselves staying as drunk as possible to assuage their interminable circumstances. The question of whether to stay or go loomed over them like a great burning eye, best kept blinded by alcohol. Sometimes they used the back rooms for sex. By and large, they did their best not to think.

They all had battles and heartaches behind them. Their souls had been blackened by grief and death and dark deeds thrust upon them by the exigencies of survival. They'd left their ethics in pools of blood and misery. They didn't know if they were evil or good; they only knew that they had become dangerous people, as evidenced by the fact that they lived.

Rapscale had been sitting by one of the west-facing windows for longer than he cared to think about. Once in a while he glanced through the scarred, mineral-encrusted panes at the view outside. He did not do this often, for the view was not interesting and never changed. Beyond lay the Endless Plain, a flat, bone-white expanse of salt-stiff-ened sand marred only by an occasional dust devil.

The last hundred or so times Rapscale had glanced out the window, his eyes had encountered naught but that endless sameness, and he expected no different result this time. Sometimes—rarely, but sometimes—people came in from the east. Nobody ever came in from the west.

He did see something different, however: a dot in the far distance, near the horizon. He blinked, assuming it was a mote in his own eye, but the dot was not exorcized. He frowned at the dot through his inebriate daze. After a long period of scrutiny, he determined that the dot was getting bigger, and decided, against all logic, that it was real.

"Someone's coming," he said.

Agnes Brightbottom looked out an east-facing window. "I don't see 'em."

"Not that way," said Rapscale.

"West?" said Agnes.

"Which way am I facing, you witless trollop?"

This exchange stirred interest among the other patrons. They gathered around Rapscale's table, and the other west-facing window, and also at the doorway between, and watched the dot gradually increase into the discernible figure of a man.

Giant Bill Grundy planted his massive fist, knuckles down, on Rapscale's table, and leaned low to peer out. "It's The Grieve," he said.

꩜

The Grieve maintained his slow, steady gait toward the Dire Disputes Saloon, it being the only sanctuary extant on the Endless Plain. He had battled through monsters and ghouls and marauders to get there. He was dehydrated and famished to the brink of death, but he kept on. His will was so alloyed with his body that, were he to expire, it would happen mid-stride. In fact his body might go a few strides farther, even dead.

The saloon was a broad, one-storey building, with a peaked tin roof and a gallery in front up a short flight of steps. The walls had been painted white, at some point, and the roof and window frames pale green. But the paint had long since oxidized and flaked, and little remained of its colors.

The Grieve saw people looking at him, out the windows and through the door. Few of their looks were friendly. The Grieve cinched his belt a notch tighter, pulled the hood of his patchwork robe forward a bit to further obscure his face. He climbed the steps, crossed the gallery, muttered "Ramshackle," and pushed through the red, swinging doors.

Most of the people inside made way. A few edged forward.

"I'm not in a killing mood," The Grieve said, and proceeded, at his steady gait, toward the bar, where the bartender awaited him. The finger bones hanging from

The Grieve's belt softly clattered, and the jawless skull on the hasp of his satchel scraped against the leather.

The others at the bar, all but one, moved away. The Grieve threw his hood back, revealing his ravaged, bearded face, crisscrossed with scars, and the hairless gap in his scalp. He leaned on the bar top. "Appox."

Appox nodded. "Alexander."

"No one calls me that anymore."

"What will you have?"

"Water. Food."

Appox gestured at a waitress, who hurried into the kitchen behind the bar. He poured a tall glass of water and pushed it toward The Grieve.

The Grieve drained the glass and glanced around. "Your premises have diminished."

"One does as one can."

The Grieve did not recognize himself in the mirror at the bar back. He extended a finger at a bottle of rotgut. Appox poured shots for them both, lifted his and said, "Absent friends."

The Grieve grunted and they drank.

"I've been waiting for you a long time," Appox said.

"Bit of a hike, following your fuckin' arrow."

"Not my arrow."

The Grieve glanced right at the only archetype still standing at the bar with him. "Must hurt, being you."

"Incessantly," the skinless man said, and downed a shot of whiskey.

"The fuck archetype are you, anyway?"

"Truth, I think."

The Grieve chuckled grimly. Veins and viscera, the untold story. "Well, you're a survivor."

"That I am," the skinless man said, patting the Liston knife sheathed at his waist.

"The archetypes have scattered," Appox said.

"Those who haven't killed each other." The Grieve grimaced at the bar's other patrons, who had resumed their tables but remained watchful. "What will humanity do without its heroes," he asked rhetorically, his tone steep with irony.

"Our ranks will replenish," the skinless man said.

The Grieve's lip curled.

Appox signaled an assistant to take over at the bar, and snagged the bottle. The Grieve followed him to a table at the back, away from the others. The waitress brought The Grieve a plate of stew and a small loaf of bread. He devoured the stew without care for its components, and mopped up with the bread.

He pushed the plate away and poured himself another shot. "Any word of Virgin or Sam?"

Appox shook his head. "How have you fared?"

"With what?"

Appox didn't answer.

"My 'quest?'"

Appox arched an eyebrow.

The Grieve sneered.

Appox cleared his throat. "Garritch has closed many doors. It has set off cascades in several parts of the Labyrinth. There is no knowing how far the damage will go or if it can be undone."

The Grieve swallowed and looked away. "Lark?"

"Garritch has four of her five aspects. The fifth remains at large, whereabouts unknown."

"Hey, Grieve!" a booming voice called.

The Grieve didn't need to look to identify the speaker. He heard Bill Grundy get up from his table and stomp towards him.

"Where'd you get that skull?" Grundy demanded.

The Grieve glanced up at Grundy's looming, eight-foot-tall frame. The giant's ten-gallon hat nearly touched the ceiling. The Grieve inclined his head west, toward the desert, in answer to his question.

"You think that's funny, making jewelry out of a guy's timbers?"

"I like bones," The Grieve said. "I needed a cup."

"Sick fuckin' bastard," said Grundy.

"Ironic, isn't it, Bill? If people'd left me alone, and let nature take its course, a lot of them would be alive and I'd be dead. Assholes keep bringing me water and food."

"I know that skull," Grundy said.

The Grieve sucked his teeth. "It has some interesting striations around the orbits."

"That's Magrod's skull. I know because I killed him. He deserves better than to ride your satchel."

"Like I said, I needed a cup."

"You've got no respect," Grundy growled.

"Respect!?" a voice cried from across the bar. Patrons parted and the voice's source was revealed to be a slim woman dressed like a cowgirl, in a leather vest and chaps, with six-shooters holstered in her gun belt, and knives sheathed on her belt. The brim of her hat dipped low, concealing her face. She stood up. "You don't know the meaning of the word, Bill Grundy."

The ambient temperature of impending conflict rose within the bar.

"I look forward to a time," Appox said to The Grieve, "when your arrival in my establishment does not herald violence."

"Wouldn't that be nice," The Grieve muttered.

The woman crossed the bar slowly, a threat in every step. Grundy drew back. The patrons of the bar gravitated surreptitiously into camps, some toward Grundy, some toward the woman, a neutral smattering staying where they were.

"The doors slam shut all around us," the cowgirl said to the crowd. "The Quick feel it happening, all through the ways of mystery and imagination." She tilted her hat back and put her hands on her hips. "From Crystalon to the Floating Realms, the vaults and the skies darken, eternity constricts to moments, what once was shared divides into arguments, and hope shrivels in the hearts of the living and the dead."

She scanned the room, holding every gaze, until her eyes met The Grieve's with a challenge.

He knew what she wanted, but he didn't have any more to give her. He'd had his fill of fighting and killing and scraping to exist. He didn't want a quest. Her eyes were a medicine he didn't want either, a balm seeping through his desiccated heart, calling him to be true.

He looked away.

Lark extended her hand at him. "One man, blind to our history, blind to his own, thrust himself blindly into the fray. He has stood for all of us, even those who stand against him, with no design in his heart but love." She glared up at Bill Grundy. "There is not one among us more deserving of respect than he."

A couple of people clapped. The Grieve poured himself another shot but Lark batted it from his hand. He snapped to his feet, inches from her face, letting her feel his ire.

She neither backed nor looked away. She removed her glove and raised her hand, palm open, toward him.

The Grieve stared at her hand. "I'm not that person," he hissed. But shame welled up in a flood.

She reached down and lifted his hand, lightly brushed her fingertips against his.

The Grieve saw the maelstrom, swirling in his mind, insisting love was a lie, that he didn't deserve it, that his soul was too ruined, that he was a twisted caricature of a semblance of a man. He didn't have a heart, he didn't have a soul, he didn't even have a self. The universe would be better off without him, along with the rest of humanity.

A spark leapt from Lark's fingers to his, and a different certainty ferreted through the darkness in The Grieve, cracking open the carapace maze that had hardened in the depths of his being. He saw what the real lie was, how he had been deceived, and how his will to love had been shackled and perverted.

He stared in Lark's aeons-deep eyes and remembered their first kiss, remembered making love with her, remembered her kneeling beside him in bed, laughing for the sheer joy of mirth. It wasn't a lie and it never had been.

It was the whole damn point of his fucking existence.

A liberating rage swelled in him. He stepped back from Lark and threw off his patchwork robe with a roar, revealing his battered armor. He drew his sword, held the hilt to his heart, and bowed his head, tears streaming from his eyes. "I serve Lark Niamh Ó Cadhla," he declared, "The High Quints, Keeper of the Five Ways and Defender of the Traveling Doors." He planted his sword in the floor and took a knee before his lady love.

Lark touched his face gently. "Get up, Sandy. I am not your Queen."

"You are Queen of my heart."

"Do you make a claim on me?"

He looked up, fearful. "No, Milady, you belong to no man."

"Nor you any woman." She held out her hand. "Rise, Knight-errant."

He took her hand and stood, her mere touch chasing fatigue from his being. For a brief moment of grace, they were together.

The moment was broken by Bill Grundy, who bellowed, "Be damned to you both!"

"Oh, hell," Appox muttered tiredly.

Grundy pulled his gun, but Rapscale snagged Grundy's wrist with his bullwhip and the shot went wide, hitting the skinless man in the shoulder.

The place erupted into chaos. The neutrals were drawn into the fray, forced to defend themselves if not their principles, except for one elder drunk, who wove his way through the flying chairs, swinging fists and gunfire to the bar, where he started to replenish his drink, but was thwarted when a bullet hit the bottle.

Close combat rendered weapons encumbrances, and the battle turned into a brawl. Sandy collapsed his sword and swung at an Asian-faced man who side-stepped, grabbed Sandy's wrist and tried to flip him, but a grey-haired dame jumped on his back and boxed his ears.

Sandy pulled free and back-handed a fat man who staggered against two women slugging it out behind him. Lark ducked between two brutes grabbing for her, swung around and punched them both in the throat. Bill Grundy knocked two men's heads together, grabbed Lark by the arm and flung her against a wall. Two gunslingers in sombreros slugged Grundy in the stomach, and he sent them both flailing through a window.

Appox fought like a dancer, bent low to knock the legs out from under a man in a Conquistador's helmet, throat-punched another in Bedouin's robes, dodged a bottle swung at his head by a burly woman in a tight-fitting tunic.

Bill Grundy swept men and women aside, making his way to Sandy. Sandy kicked him in the groin, which only made Grundy glare at him balefully. Rapscale swung his bullwhip at Grundy but this time Grundy caught it, yanked Rapscale to him and sent him crashing into the mirror behind the bar.

A siren screech split the air and everyone stopped. Through a broken window at the front of the bar, Sandy saw a vast shadow rush towards them across the Plain.

Faceless, oily-black soldiers with burning eyes emerged from the shadow and ran en masse toward the entrance. Behind them, a wavering distortion in the desert air, like a mirage, resolved into the figure of Garritch, who strolled nonchalantly behind his enchanted troops. The horde of ur-men poured into the bar and the fighting resumed, more lethally. The ur-soldiers slew all in their path, showing no consideration for allies.

Grundy seized Sandy by the throat and lifted him high, shouting in his face, "See what you've done?"

Lark climbed on Grundy's back and clawed at his eyes. He released Sandy and clutched for Lark, who swung from his neck, dodging his groping hands. Grundy lost his balance and fell backwards against the northern wall of the bar. The wall collapsed outward and the roof sank with a creaking groan.

Sandy unfolded his sword and hewed into Garritch's minions. Gunfire resumed and the floor grew slick with ichor and blood. Sandy fought toward Garritch, who stood calmly in the entrance, observing the mayhem. Most of the patrons of the bar who had been fighting each other united against the ur-soldiers. Garritch locked eyes with Sandy and grinned.

The walls were so shot with holes and hewn with blows that their load-bearing strength began to fail and the roof creaked toward collapse. The contest spilled onto the Plain.

Sandy saw Lark overmatched, surrounded by ur-soldiers, and left off striving toward Garritch. He fought through the Quick and the dead to achieve her side. Appox joined them. The three of them fought a growing circle of ur-soldiers, who were hampered in having to climb over growing piles of the fallen.

Sandy did not see the blow coming. He thrust his blade through an ur-soldier and turned to meet Bill Grundy's gargantuan fist, smashing into him like a hammer. Sandy fell back, dazed, and felt something pierce his gut, looked down to see a smoking hole in the armor shielding his abdomen.

In the seconds before he lost consciousness, he saw the battle around him on the Plain. He watched the skinless man leap at Garritch and be cast aside in a splatter of guts. The Dire Pursuits Saloon collapsed into rubble. Sandy felt his sword's power leave him. It retracted into a caliper in his hand, and his armor disintegrated. He saw Lark, a knife in both hands, leap high at Bill Grundy and sink both blades in his chest.

He felt Appox's arms around him, and then saw nothing at all.

Chapter Twenty-two

Alexander awoke on a large bed in a softly lit chamber, sweet, cool air wafting across his face. He lay beneath covers pulled up to his throat with his head resting deep in a pillow. Above him a pale white canopy ruffled faintly.

He turned his head toward the light and met a vision of marvels. Broad archways opened onto a loggia bordered by spiral columns and balusters. Beyond lay a city of crystal towers and giant trees as tall and taller than the buildings, amid which flew steam and propeller-powered blimps and balloons, flying platforms that seemed held aloft by magic, and myriad other strange crafts. The enormous branches of the trees were lined with houses. Hazy in the distance, terraced farms climbed the wall of a cavern.

Sandy tried to sit up and felt a warm hand on his shoulder.

"Gently, Knight-errant. Your wounds are yet mending."

A woman of serene mien sat beside him on the bed. She had long, golden braids, and wore upon her brow a living diadem grown with tiny leaves of many kinds and colors, centered by an opalescent oval stone.

"Where am I?" he asked.

"You are in Crystalon. I am Althea, Queen of this realm, and you are in my care."

The woman helped Sandy sit up, then turned to a man in a white gown who bore a bowl on a tray. She took the bowl and fed Sandy a spoonful of broth that tasted of mushrooms and vegetables. He swallowed and closed his eyes. The broth felt good going down.

"Milady," he said, embarrassed, "I can feed myself."

The Queen smiled. "There is healing in letting oneself be served, Knight-errant. Accept succor. Your heart has need of it."

Sandy let the Queen feed him. He managed only a few spoonfuls before his stomach would take no more.

Althea gave the bowl to her retainer. "You have lain many days on the verge of death," she told Sandy. "Your wounds were grievous and nearly claimed you."

"How did I get here?"

"Appox brought you. He forsook his establishment to quicken you to safety."

"And Lark?"

The Queen's expression saddened. "Garritch holds sway over all of her aspects. He keeps them separate and occludes their minds. He means to weaken them until he can turn them to his purpose."

Sandy turned away. A tear leaked from his eye.

"Abjure despair, Alexander. The ministries of the Quick are not yet exhausted, and your friends are with you." She gestured at someone. Tall doors opened; Virgin, Sam and Appox, entered and came to Sandy's side.

"How you doing, pal?" Sam asked.

For a moment Sandy was too overcome to speak. "Better now," he managed, and gave Appox a grateful nod.

Sandy didn't feel he deserved the esteem he saw in Virgin's eyes. She bore her nakedness, as ever, with dignity. She lifted her chin, holding his gaze, summoning him to the moment.

He cleared his throat. "Don't you ever get cold?"

"Not in Crystalon, thankfully." She grinned. "Disappointed?"

"You want me to lie?" The others laughed; Sandy was too weak to do more than grin. "I wasn't sure Thracia would let you go," he said to Virgin and Sam.

"She's all right, when you get to know her," Sam said.

"She's lonely. People should visit her, once in awhile."

"Let him rest now," Althea said.

Appox gripped Sandy's arm and Virgin kissed him on the forehead. Sam tipped his hat.

Sandy spent the next two Labyrinthine cycles of day and night resting and getting his strength back. His clothes were brought to him, mended and cleaned, along with his map and wallet and vernier caliper. The crude robe and satchel he had fashioned on the Endless Plain, along with his finger-bone belt and Magrod's jawless skull, were brought to him, too. He asked that the robe and satchel be destroyed, and the bones retired with respect.

He bathed and shaved, stood awhile examining himself in the mirror. The scars on his face, arms, legs, back and chest had become less pronounced. The stitches that had closed the wound in his stomach had been removed.

Two of Althea's retainers, a man and a woman, led him through the corridors of the palace to an open air platform crowded with travelers, where he was met by the Queen and his friends.

The view from the platform was breathtaking. The crystal spires and tree villages of Crystalon extended into the vastness of the cavern, a world unto its own. To the right rose the wall of the cavern opposite the one visible from his room. It was nearer, and Sandy could see people working in the farms, and loading harvested produce onto blimps. The most astonishing thing, though, was the titanic tree at the city's heart. With a bone-white trunk and limbs, and billowing, cloud-like masses of turquoise leaves, it towered above all else.

"The World Tree," Althea said. "Its roots extend throughout the Labyrinth, and link with its counterpart in the Mirror Realm."

A train whistle sounded, and a flying locomotive pulled up and stopped with a loud burst of steam. Doors opened and conductors hopped off, lowering steps for those disembarking and boarding. Althea, Sandy and his companions boarded the lead car, which bore the Queen's multi-foliar emblem.

The train pulled away from the platform. Sandy watched the fantastic city pass by through the windows. The train veered toward the World Tree, and eventually it filled the view. The tree's branches supported a city of their own, lined with homes great and small. Hosts of flying vehicles wove among the branches.

The train stopped at a platform on the tree's trunk about halfway up from its base. They disembarked and crossed to a tall entryway. Attendants waiting by the open doors preceded them down a long corridor, deep into the heartwood of the tree. The pearlescent wood of the walls was polished to glossy smoothness.

At the end of the corridor they entered a domed chamber, in the center of which hung a giant, three-dimensional holographic map. A gallery of seats, all vacant at present, encircled the hologram, and below them a low barrier defined the perimeter of a sunken arena. The group descended a flight of stairs between the seats. At the bottom, a large woman in coveralls, holding a tall staff, stood looking into the arena.

She turned as they approached. Her face was deeply creased with age and she was missing an eye. She did not wear an eyepatch; Sandy could see inside the empty socket.

"My Queen," the woman said. A desiccated nodule of flesh hung from her staff by a slim cord.

"Niralia." Althea introduced Sandy and his friends.

Sandy stared up at the holographic map.

"Behold the Labyrinth," Althea said.

It resembled a teardrop-shaped cloud. Althea suggested Sandy take a circuit around the map, to see the Labyrinth from all sides. Within the amorphous, shifting maze, a few features were static. One of them, at its upper end, was Crystalon, marked by a green dot and its name. Throughout the map innumerable passages looped and twisted like a mess of unspooled string. A kind of broken, elliptical disk bisected the map vertically, bordered by the words, "Endless Plain." The overall structure of the Labyrinth was incomprehensibly complex.

Sandy completed the circuit, returning to Althea and his friends. "I think I could study this thing for a lifetime and not understand it."

"A great many scholars do exactly that," Althea said. "This map, vague as it is, is the result of the efforts of thousands, over the course of millennia." She waved her hand and innumerable blue dots shone throughout the hologram. "These are the doors of quickening, those that are fixed and have been identified. Many times their number are in a state of perpetual movement, impossible to assign location." She waved her hand again and the majority of the blue dots turned red. "These are doors Garritch has closed. He has closed more that travel."

Sandy shook his head. "How is he doing this?"

"All I have been able to divine is that he has learned to manipulate primal matter. His art is beyond me. He concentrates on the anchoring doors. When enough anchors are shut in a given area, a cascade results, and the other doors shut there as well. We protect a number of anchoring doors in Crystalon, so that we do not become isolated. But his sorcery will find them eventually."

"If he can do this, why does he need Lark?"

"Because everything is connected. The Quints bonded herself to the Five Doors, five of the most powerful and stable anchoring doors in the entire Labyrinth. She bonded her soul to them. By doing so she exerts a countering influence that affects the entire Labyrinth. When Garritch first started closing doors, most of them reopened almost immediately. Why I don't know, and I don't think he does either. He became convinced, though, that The Quints had something to do with it. Obviously, he was right. Every time he enthralled one of her aspects, the percentage of doors he closed that stayed closed increased, as did his ability to manifest cascades. And, there is this." Althea gestured again, and images appeared, superimposed over the map, of caverns in which the walls were crumbling and deteriorating, some above cities.

"Closing doors is causing this?" Sandy asked.

"We have no other explanation," Althea said.

Sandy puffed out a breath. "What do you want from me?"

"We can't do anything if we don't know where Garritch is keeping The Quints. He has hidden her from us completely. We had hoped that, because of your special connection with her, you might succeed in finding her where we have failed. The fact that the Hierophant facilitated your entry to the Labyrinth strengthened that hope. But the situation has become dire. We can no longer wait to see. That is why I brought you here. Do you sense anything, looking at the map, that might lead us to Garritch?"

Sandy looked again. "Where is Earth?"

Althea gestured, and a bright blue globe appeared at the narrow tip of the tear-drop cloud. "The Earth is at the juncture between the Labyrinth and the Mirror Realm of the dead."

Sandy had been so focused on the holographic image that he had not looked into the arena beneath it. The floor of the arena was made of polished black stone upon which a two-dimensional rendering of the map showed. A man in jeans, a work shirt and boots slowly traversed its surface holding two L-shaped rods with the long ends straight out before him.

"Ben is Niralia's husband," Althea said. "He is the best diviner in the realm. He seeks the location of the Citadel of the Maimed, Garritch's stronghold. He's been looking for a long time."

Sandy looked back and forth between the two-dimensional map and the hologram. "What do you mean, 'Mirror Realm?' Are you saying there's a negative Labyrinth?"

"Not in any contrary sense, but in the polar sense, yes." Althea gestured at the map again, and it shrank to make room for an inverted tear-drop-shaped hologram, the same size as the map of the Labyrinth, positioned above it with the Earth in-between. The inverted tear-drop was completely opaque, without any features discernible in its hazy volume.

Ben shouted from the arena. The Mirror Labyrinth had manifested on the floor there as well. The diviner strode onto it. As he neared the center of its inscrutable area, his rods crossed. He looked up at Althea.

Althea's expression sagged. "Are you certain?" she asked Ben.

The diviner nodded at the crossed bars. "There is no question, Milady."

"We never imagined it," Althea said.

"Imagined what?" Sandy asked. "What does it mean?"

"Tell me exactly what the Hierophant told you," Althea asked somberly.

"He said that I had to cross the Endless Plain, and forget who I am in order to find out who I am. He said I would need a talisman to help me remember myself." Sandy pulled out the vernier caliper and showed it to Althea. "Lark said something like that, too."

Althea studied the implement. Her lips twisted with chagrin.

"What?" Sandy asked.

"I was foolish not to consult with you sooner. I did not want to bias your decisions. I think I understand, now, what the Hierophant intended. Garritch has hidden in the realm of the dead."

CHAPTER TWENTY-THREE

A shocking din, like a massive rupture of stone, broke through the map room from outside. The group hurried up the stairs and down the hall to investigate. Nearing the outer entrance they heard a rising tumult of voices.

They reached the platform. The number of vehicles in the air had multiplied. People crowded on the World Tree's limbs, straining to see through the dense, turquoise foliage.

Althea whistled, and a flying white disc sailed down to them. She boarded and beckoned the others to accompany her. Niralia and Ben joined them.

The disc had no barrier around its perimeter; its surface held Sandy's feet with a steadying force. The contrivance bore them out through the branches, dodging among the other vehicles vying for passage.

They cleared the World Tree's canopy and saw immediately the source of alarm: a darkening, like a great bruise, spreading across the right-hand wall of the cavern. The terraced farms within its boundary were disintegrating.

"This is what I feared," Althea said.

"What's happening?" Sandy asked.

"The Labyrinth is like a great mind," Appox said. "When a mind closes, it constricts and ossifies."

"That has to be an oversimplification," Sandy objected.

"It's an apt analogy." Althea extended her hands and closed her eyes. A power emanated from her. Sandy couldn't see it but he felt it—an oscillation coursing across his skin. The darkening of the cavern wall slowed and ceased to expand.

"I cannot stop it," Althea said, "only impede its spread. I had hoped to spare you this, Knight-errant. I must ask you to return to the Endless Plain and complete your crossing."

Sandy stared at her. "You've got to be joking."

Althea shook her head. "Sadly not. We have to act quickly, before all of the doors close."

"But that—" Sandy pointed back toward the map room—"I saw on the map, that thing extends across the entire *Labyrinth*. That's an area, what, hundreds, thousands of times greater than the surface of the Earth? You expect me to *cross* that?"

"The map is conceptual. No one knows the dimensions of the Plain, only that it extends, in some manner, through all the reaches of the Labyrinth. But the Plain is also a maze. You will have to lose yourself, Alexander, to find your way. If you wish to save the Quints, and stop the catastrophe you see unfolding here from worsening beyond remedy, you will have to forget yourself, and shed all you know as your history—"

"Aw, *Jesus*, you people and your fucking *riddles!* All the fucking *gobbledygook—no!* No, no, no. No *way* am I going back there."

"Alexander, this destruction could spread throughout the Labyrinth. It could spread to the Earth itself."

"How the fuck does that become *my* responsibility? Why don't *you* go? *Any* of you people understand this better than I do! This is how things work? Some random schmuck gets yanked out of nowhere, and everything lands on *me?* 'You must.' The *hell* I must!"

"I know this is hard to understand—"

"It's *impossible* to understand!"

Sandy stared beseechingly at his friends. They wouldn't look at him. They all wanted—*needed*—him to do this, return to that endless hell of salt and sand and kill and kill and kill. They weren't just asking him to die, they were asking him to torture himself to death. "You're crazy! You're all crazy!" He gestured helplessly at the wounded cavern wall. "You think I can *stop* that? I can't! It's not *in* me! I'm telling you! I *know!*"

Sam gripped his arm. "You don't know what you can do, pal."

Sandy searched Sam's eyes for any faltering certainty, any out. He pulled away, looked at the others. "But—but we *know* where Garritch is …"

Virgin took him in her arms.

"There's no map of the Mirror Realm," Ben said. "It's as vast as the Labyrinth here."

"There are forces at work beyond the scope of the rational mind," Althea said.

"You're asking me to go mad."

"I'm asking you to find the sanity at the heart of madness, in the core of your being."

"Give him a moment," Virgin said, "all of you."

Sandy, limp and trembling in Virgin's arms, looked out on Crystalon and all of its stirring wonders—he wanted to stay here, live here forever with Lark. No one should be asked to do what they were asking of him.

He noticed Ben and Niralia watching him, holding hands. He didn't think he'd ever seen a woman uglier than Niralia, especially with that missing eye, and yet the love and caring her husband felt for her, and she for him, was obvious. Ben's love for Niralia showed in the ease with which he stood by her, and the warmth in his compassionate smile. For a moment Sandy saw her through his eyes: what a place of grace it must be, to dwell in the path of her love.

The terrible knowledge that he would do what they asked sank through him, and he felt himself bow to fate. God, the universe, whatever, had pointed its finger at him, and there was no dodging its infernal digit. If this was his only chance to see Lark again, he would take it. He seized

Virgin, clinging to her as one would a mother, sheltering in the warmth of her flesh, and fought to master his terror.

Niralia held his gaze with her one eye. He saw her kindness, and understood something more about beauty, how it transformed over time, and matured the perception of the ardent beholder.

"Your love will lead to your love," she said quietly.

Her voice as much as her words steadied Sandy. He patted Virgin's back. "I'm okay," he whispered, "I'm okay."

She released him slowly, rubbed his shoulders, wiped his eyes.

Sandy puffed out a long breath. "Sorry, everyone."

His companions all regarded him with caring. They did not want this fate for him. Any one of them would take his place if they could. The world was falling apart. He remembered Lark gazing down at him in their bedroom among the stars, the laughter in her angelic, burning eyes, and he surrendered to the will of the universe. He nodded to Althea.

"You will have to relinquish your talisman," she told him.

"How am I supposed to defend myself?"

"It will not be that kind of crossing."

Sandy laughed scoffingly. "Well, I'm glad to hear you say so, and I hope you know what you're talking about, but," he shook his head, "Cabal told me I'll need it to remember myself."

"Yes, but you cannot forget yourself while it is in your possession."

Sandy grimaced. "You better be right, or it's going to be a short crossing."

She gestured at Sam, Appox and Virgin. "Choose a custodian to keep it for you."

Appox met his gaze with an intense appeal in his eyes.

Sandy gave him the caliper.

Appox secured it in an inner pocket of his jacket. "I will bring it to you in your moment of need. I swear it on my life."

"I'll hold you to that." Sandy worked his tongue in his mouth. There'd been enough drama in the last ten minutes to last him forever.

Virgin placed her hand on his heart. "We'll be there when you need us."

Sam grabbed his hand and shook it.

Sandy turned to Althea. "Okay, I guess."

"Remember this, Alexander Creaze, Knight-errant of the Quints, Defender of the Traveling Doors and anointed archetype of the Secret Realms—remember it as long as you can. It is not the Endless Plain you cross but the chasm of your innermost being. I set you upon your path with a hope and a prayer, and all the blessings given me to bestow."

Althea flicked her hand at Sandy, the world warped, and he found himself again surrounded by an endless expanse of sand.

Chapter Twenty-four

No food, no water, no compass or indication of direction, and millions, billions, trillions of square miles of flat, hardened sand. To 'cross.'

Althea had implied that was a kind of metaphor, that he had to cross the chasm of his innermost being, whatever that meant.

Maybe it was as well to stay put, then. Not wear himself out in the heat.

He pulled out his map. Only two features appeared: the word *'Plain,'* writ large, and an arrow pointing the way he was facing.

Not stay put, then. He'd ignored the map's advice once, and nearly drowned. He put the map in his pocket and started walking.

No assembly of eldritch warriors barred his way this time. He remembered the fights he'd survived. Marauders of many stripes had quickened onto the Plain to deter him, to kill him. From their blood-soaked garments he'd fashioned his patchwork robe.

He'd thought that had been the stripping away of his being the Hierophant had intended. With each confrontation he'd felt less recognizable to himself, particularly as he came to see that a part of him liked it. He'd assumed that his reflexes for kindness and decency were innate to his character, but under them was a deeper instinct for survival, a willingness to end lives to preserve his own, to take the water and food of his adversaries, and find satisfaction in their failures.

It mystified him, why so many had journeyed to the Plain to challenge him. Agents of Garritch, he'd assumed, seeking to curry favor with the presumptive victor of an existential conflict. Sandy had become the storied loner of legend, the beleaguered hero with the sole capacity to overcome a wicked foe.

In truth he didn't know the motives of the men he'd fought. He only knew that with each one he killed a piece of him darkened, and his cynicism increased.

He'd undertaken his quest in the name of love. That love had turned to ash, fighting his way across the Endless Plain. He hadn't let the others see it. To them he was still 'Sandy,' the love-struck fool who'd thrown his life away for a kiss. But that person had died the death of a thousand cuts.

He did not know himself anymore.

The image of Lark still called up feelings of love and devotion, but the image had weathered, fading in memory.

And yet, the moment he'd seen her again, in the Dire Disputes Saloon, the confirmation of love had poured through him like an elixir.

In her absence, confronted with relentless violence and hardship, he'd had to stop thinking about her. His ordeal on the Plain had yielded to a single motivating force: the will to endure. He remembered coming upon fields of bones, where forgotten battles had been fought for nameless reasons, completing the assembly of his robes, fashioning his gruesome belt.

"We come to fight The Grieve."

One opponent he'd let live. He remembered crouching over the bested youth, telling him of the death he'd dealt, how he'd seen his opponents grieve, in their dying moments, their decisions to confront him. It had been in their eyes, every one. Somehow, then, he didn't know how, he sent him away. He looked in the young, desperate eyes and knew the boy couldn't quicken himself, so he did it for him.

Sandy stopped walking. Somehow, he'd opened a door and sent the boy through it. The ability to do so had come from a deep, instinctive part of himself that he didn't understand. If he could do that for another, he ought to be able to do it for himself.

He had no idea how.

None of the people he'd fought had been able to escape, he realized. It was obvious. If they had they would have done so. What person, on the threshold of death, does not take any other exit available? One might die in defense of family or comrades, but the adversaries he'd encountered on the Plain, men or monsters, had had no such allegiances.

Sandy recognized now what he had not had the latitude to see before: the grim resignation in all who'd stood against him. They'd had no alternative than fight or die, and come expecting to be killed.

Distraction.

Things had happened out of sequence. He'd never been meant to cross the Plain in possession of his talisman. Or maybe he had. Maybe all of those battles had been moves in a chess match between the Hierophant and Garritch.

It didn't matter, now. That was not the way of this journey. Sandy looked at the map and it was as it had been, with a single arrow pointing ahead.

His only contest now was with himself.

Hardest to look back on was the carnage he'd left at the entrance to the Plain. He'd turned that cave into a charnel house. Now he saw that assailants had been set before him to give *him* no choice but to fight.

Distraction.

It was still distraction. If he carried forward that burden of guilt, if he let himself remain blighted with regret, it would kill him. He would never complete this crossing so encumbered. He had to pardon himself for his own ignorance, for killing in defense of his life. He had to overcome doubt of his motives.

His life had been composed of moments that seemed linked together by ineluctable inevitability. But that was all memory, and memory was flawed. It deteriorated and left hints of the past, like fossils. One thing remembered, another forgotten, with no indication how the determination had been made, in the creases of the brain, to cling to one and relinquish another. The past, assumed and relied upon, reinforced by habit and one's relations with others, in fact inhabited a fog. People were forgotten. *'Hi, Sandy, remember me? We took that hike in the Adirondacks? That stuff you said changed my life ...'* Not a clue who that was. Couldn't see her face.

And what of dreams? They, too, were a history, forgotten unless one exercised oneself to remember them, or they were so extraordinary, as Gordon's had been, that they secured their own territory in consciousness. Some people lost their memories entirely in decrepitude, and their loved ones said it was like losing the person they'd known. But there was still a person there, stopping and blinking and wondering where they were.

Beginnings and endings, one thing started, another finished, and the isolate being traveled a chosen course through limitless uncertainty, anchored by concepts, memories and beliefs selected as anchors to secure life to a place in time. All relinquished at death, and what happened then was unknowable, hidden, defined by theory or belief as nothing or something or indeterminate.

Underneath all that was the persistence of consciousness, which existed with or without memory, irrespective of belief. Sandy trudged across the Plain, its unknowable dimensions echoing the profound lassitude of a binding grief, that all one could ever know or learn was irremediably encompassed by ignorance. The drawers upon drawers of bones he had sorted and catalogued were grains in an hourglass, filtered down to him by creatures whose lives had been lost to the winds of time. Their experiences, what they'd known of the world, how they had accommodated themselves to existence had been reduced to the conjectures of the researchers who unearthed them, and whose uncertainties, in turn, would be left to the conjectures of others yet to come. His own history was but a particle in a consuming void.

And yet he remained conscious and his experience of reality seemed infinite and eternal, a lesser infinity within one unimaginably greater.

Below that—what was below that? Was anything below that? All the moments of his life that he could recall were ephemeral dust, fictional in their essential makeup because he reshaped them as time moved on. Some people remembered events from movies more clearly than their own lives. Misremembered, too, as they discovered re-watching films seen years before. *That didn't happen like that, did it? That character didn't say that.* All through the serpentine vagaries of sentience, a wish bound by a prayer, that the self existed and life mattered. That there was a way into the future for both the living and the dead, and the individual's experience retained value.

If only to the others one knew and cared about, however ephemeral their mutual accord. Sandy opened himself to the fiction of his life, and the particles of his identity slipped from him, his history relinquished to the tide of a recurrent question: Who or what was he in the absence of a life?

He had been born, and he did not remember the event. His fiction had begun sometime later, when his memories began to anchor themselves to a personal history. But there was a deeper history, in the vast unknowing. He had only vague impressions of it, affixed to the understanding of the universe granted his individual psyche.

The Plain extended about him, infinite in all directions; it had no boundary. It was the gulf between him and an unnameable desire. A fathomless chasm opened in the salt-sand before him; he did not know if it was inside or outside of his mind or both. On the far side stood Lark, windblown and ravishing in her unexplainable attraction. Between them, suspended over the void, was a kind of gate—invisible but Sandy knew it was there, and he knew that on the other side existed the pure substance of consciousness, unanchored to history or any species of awareness with which he was familiar. He was drawn toward it by a hypothetical arrow on a featureless map.

He surrendered to the certainty of loss.

He stepped out onto the chasm. As he walked across its nothingness, the vestiges of his identity fell from him. He passed through the invisible gate, and in a great flood remembered other lives, as men and women and creatures of other worlds. He could not hold the memories or process them—they were an ocean, changeless and never the same. He was drawn through them with a celerity unmeasurable outside of its own context—it could have been millennia or the blink of an eye. And he became aware of a great mind with a mighty intent, and in the presence of that mind he was torn into particles and a terror overcame him that everything was destroyed and recreated with each gesture, each step, each breath.

Lark stood before him in the primordial firmament. He no longer knew her but he recognized her; he no longer recognized her but he knew her, and his spirit effervesced with the memory of a kiss. He felt the intention of the great mind, to express that which had not yet been expressed, and fill the void of unknowing, both to reveal truth and create it.

Lark's visage filled his mind's eye. There was no explaining her beauty, no why or wherefore, only the truth of love, the word made flesh, the fiction made fact. Sandy fell to his knees and wept, he knew not why. A certainty with the character of grace assured him that he was right in some hope he possessed that he could not name.

He came back to himself. His memories were a knot, secreted in the cosmos of his being. He did not need to know who he was; in that moment the knowledge *that* he was inhabited him with a will.

From the distance came a horseman.

Chapter Twenty-five

The man who had been christened Alexander, who had been known to his friends as Sandy, and unwittingly become Knight-errant of the Quints, possessed no memory of those matters as he approached the man on horseback. He felt the Plain all around him and inside of him, indecipherable and beyond measure, contained in an infinitely vaster expression of consciousness.

The man on the black horse wore a scarf wrapped around his head, exposing only his eyes. He unwrapped the scarf, revealing a heavily bearded face and a knurled forehead.

"I know you," said the empty man.

"Aye, laddie, that you do," said the rider, "though you do not remember me."

The man full of stars stood silent, regarding the rider, waiting for what would come.

"Althea sent me to meet you. You have crossed the Endless Plain."

"One cannot cross that which has no limit."

"Such are the mysteries. And yet you've done it, and your ordeal upon the sands is over. It's time for you to be moving on, into the nether lands, to continue your quest."

"I know of no quest."

"Aye, and yet you have one. And you know I speak true."

The man full of stars looked within and saw a woman's comely countenance beckoning, and knew it called from the center of his being.

"I love her, too," said the rider, "but she chose you."

"I know nothing of being chosen."

"Aye, that's sure, and perhaps that's the wrong word, spoken in haste for I am jealous. But I'll not have my wants burden others, and it's sure, too, that I was wrong. You are the Knight-errant, laddie, and I'll be begging your pardon for doubting you."

The man full of stars did not know how to respond, so remained silent.

The rider peered across the plain. "Right, enough banter. Best be moving you along."

The man full of nothing replied, "I do not know what to do or where to go."

"That's the way of it, for the present. Your memory will return in due time. Until then, trust your map."

"Map?"

"Check your pockets."

The no-man patted himself. In the breast pocket of his jacket something crinkled. He pulled out a folded sheet of paper and opened it. It bore a single arrow, pointing downward at the dotted outline of a trapezoid. He held it up to the rider. "This?"

The rider nodded. "Trust it, for it knows your heart. It'll see you true." He withdrew a rod with a hook on its end from his robes, and pulled on the hook. The rod telescoped into a long pole. He stabbed it into the sand, snagged something and pulled. A rectangular trap door opened in the desert floor, within its frame a blackness.

The no-man looked at the map. The arrow now pointed at a solid black trapezoid. He looked uncertainly at the rider.

"I cannot say what lies beyond," the rider said. "Only one empty of memories may pass this way."

No-man sought within and understood that this was his way.

"You are our beacon now, Knight-errant," the rider said. "When you find Garritch and his wretched Citadel, we will come to you. You have my word on it, and Queen Althea's, and all who seek open consort with the stars."

No-man understood nothing of the rider's words, save that he spoke the truth as he knew it. No-man stepped through the trap door, and plummeted into nothingness.

Chapter Twenty-six

No-man fell through nothing, and contemplated empti-ness. He knew peace and freedom from wanting. He could give himself to that peace, and it might last forever. But he recognized that he was a conscious being, and that within consciousness existed a purpose supplied with a will.

Inherent in that purpose was a desire for self-knowl-edge, which required a history, and he had none. He supposed it fell to him to acquire a history, which would be an act of creation and discovery.

He knew he had crossed a great distance and met a horseman, and that a greater personal history existed before that, which he did not recall. He knew that he had a map and an arrow and that he had willingly leapt into void. He knew that he was known to some by a name—'Knight-errant'—though that seemed also to be some kind of title.

Also he knew the way of words, which meant that he had learned them, though he did not recall having done so. And he knew that something in him recognized truth.

These things, then, were the start of a new history. He was a being known as the Knight-errant, who had undertaken a quest, in the course of which he had surrendered his memory, apparently per design.

The void broke apart, torn with flags of indigo. The indigo banished the void, and he found himself falling through starless sky. From the distance below things rose toward him; the ingredients of a reality stirred into being. Some were like levitating islands, adrift in an absent sea, others resolved into winged beings.

Four of the latter, naked, two men and two women, with wings like dragonflies, flew to him and arrested his fall, catching him in their arms. They were gentle and he felt secure in their charge.

"Welcome to Levitania," said one of the females. "We have been waiting for you, Alexander."

Alexander. So he was known by another name, and was expected and welcome in this place. His new history was unfolding.

They bore him toward the floating islands, upon which were clustered elegant buildings with graceful spires, and amid their ways were emerald pools and streams and gardens.

Other beings flew about the flying cities, some with wings like those who carried him, others with flowing, multicolored wings like butterflies.

Alexander's bearers set him down gently on a broad avenue paved with vermillion cobbles and bordered by plants with leaves of many colors and luminous blooms with scents that summoned ease. At the end of the avenue rose a cerulean palace, with spires like a cathedral. Several beings descended on foot, with their wings folded, from the arched entrance of the palace, and approached him. One bore a long staff from which hung a standard woven with concentric patterns and a flower like a chrysanthemum at its center. It seemed none of the denizens of this place covered their bodies. Alexander felt conspicuous clothed.

Behind the standard bearer and his attendants two beings emerged from the palace in flight. Their wings were like enormous, flowing veils, greater and more colorful than those of any other. On their brows they wore crowns of bejeweled gold lacework.

The standard bearer knocked the end of his staff on the cobbles and said, "Calix and Ossia, King and Queen of Levitania." He bowed to Alexander and stepped aside.

Instinct bade Alexander take a knee and bow as Calix and Ossia settled to the ground before him.

"Rise, human," said the King, "your quest is known to us, and has our alliance."

The King and Queen of Levitania emanated mystical power, and in their miens resided calm and timeless wisdom.

"What know you of the fairy realm?" Ossia asked Alexander.

"Nothing," he answered.

"And of yourself?" asked Calix.

"Very little: only that I met a horseman on a plain of sand, and fell through void to come here. Also that I possess language, and am not newly born. My memories of my life before are lost to me."

"That is as it must be," said Calix. "No human may enter the fairy realm in corpus with knowledge of his past. This place exists outside of space and time. What do you seek?"

"My way," answered Alexander.

Ossia smiled at him. "He is noble and true, Calix."

"Perhaps," said the King, "but he may not linger."

"Can you tell me nothing of my quest?" Alexander asked.

"Levitania is outside of the Labyrinth," Calix said. "Still, matters there concern us. You seek one who dwells in darkness. He has violated the boundary between the living and the dead, seeking to isolate the human realm from the cosmos. He does not understand what he does, nor the consequences. He imagines himself bold but is ruled by fear, and therefore are his eyes occluded. If his vision cannot be cleared, his devices must be broken."

"How do I do that?"

"The method you will have to discover," said Ossia. "The ways of the living are known to the dead. But the ways of the dead may not be known to the living."

Alexander saw that many others had gathered about, and looked upon him with sobriety and hope. "Is this place threatened?" he asked.

"All realms suffer," answered the King, "when the measures of fear hold sway."

"Why am I here?"

"To enter the Mirror Labyrinth, in the realm of the dead. It is within our power to grant you passage," said Calix. "Do you wish it?"

"I do," said Alexander. It was the only answer in his mind.

"First quench your thirst and nourish yourself," the Queen said. She signaled one of her subjects, and he filled a goblet from a pool by the path. He brought the goblet to Alexander and held it out to him.

"Drink," said Ossia, "and be refreshed."

Alexander accepted the goblet. The fluid it contained gave off a blue luminance. He sipped it, and found that it tasted only of cool, crisp water. He discovered his thirst and drank all the goblet held.

The Queen plucked a flower like a blue chrysanthemum from a plant with broad purple leaves by the path and gave it to Alexander. "Eat."

Alexander nibbled a petal from the flower. It filled his mouth with a refreshing astringency that stirred his hunger. He consumed the flower down to its stem and belched.

The onlookers laughed and he laughed with them. Weariness overcame him, and his legs grew weak. Ossia caught him in her arms, and wrapped her wings about him. "Sleep, Knight-errant," she said. "Travel well, and may you find peace in your dreams."

CHAPTER TWENTY-SEVEN

Alexander awoke looking up into darkness, a hard, smooth surface beneath him. He sat up and found himself on a boundless plain of glass that glimmered faintly. In the distance, the encompassing darkness had a faint, grey cast.

He discovered a young boy, in a waistcoat and ascot, sitting beside him. Curled in the boy's lap was a sleeping dachshund.

A name came to Alexander. "Gordon?"

The boy smiled. "Hello, Sandy."

Sandy. That was his name, too, somehow derived from Alexander.

"I know you, but I do not remember you."

"We were friends," Gordon said, "and so we remain."

Sandy looked around. "Where are we?"

"You've crossed into the realm of the dead, my son."

Sandy rested his arms on his knees. "I wish I understood something."

"What?"

"Anything."

Gordon smiled. "You're looking for your young woman. Her name is Lark."

Sandy again saw a woman's face in his mind. It caused a constriction in his chest. "She's in danger."

"She is," Gordon said calmly, "but her chances are better, now."

Sandy frowned at Gordon. "Aren't you a bit young to be calling me son?"

Gordon grinned. "It's a matter of perspective. In the life you've forgotten I was your senior." Gordon scooted the dachshund from his lap and stood up. As he rose he grew in height and age.

"Neat trick," Sandy said. He noted an element of personality asserting itself in him.

"Age has little relevance, here." Gordon helped Sandy to his feet. "Others are waiting." He indicated a direction. "Shall we go?"

"Lead on, MacDuff."

Gordon laughed. "That's the spirit."

They set off across the plain. Sandy noticed that the glass underfoot was transparent. Star fields and galaxies were faintly visible through it. The firmament above was featureless.

"How have you been?" Gordon asked.

"Mystified, of late. Before that I suppose okay." It was good to have the company of a friend, even if he didn't remember him.

"I'm sorry I died on you. That was inconsiderate of me."

"Could you have done anything to prevent it?"

"I'm not sure. It's possible I ducked when I should have dodged."

The dachshund yipped.

Sandy glanced down. "Dog seems to agree."

"Horace is still irritated with me. He liked his spot by the window."

"Where are we going?"

"You'll see. It's a bit of a hike but we'll be there soon enough."

"Thanks for coming to meet me."

"My pleasure, dear boy."

"Not sure what I'd have done if I'd woken up here alone."

"You'd have found your way. Ah, here, we're on approach."

A vast field of bones stretched before them, parted by a narrow defile.

"Something about this is familiar," Sandy said. "I think I've been somewhere like this before."

"Not like this," Gordon said.

Sandy scrutinized the bones. He recognized many, and knew the names of the creatures to which they belonged. But there were others that were unfamiliar.

The path led towards a light, which resolved into the entrance of a passage.

"Sandy, our time is short, and I want to tell you something," Gordon said as they walked. "For love to flourish, one must yield to curiosity to see where it might go. It is possible to deny love, and shy from it, or simply wait for it to diminish in intensity until it no longer matters."

They neared the threshold, which was trimmed with bones. The prospect beyond was indistinct.

"Love is mysterious because it bothers the intellect and cannot be bound by reason or words. Scientists do no service when they strive to reduce it. Love does not belong to the lover; it is selfless. It spills outward, and graces all in its path." Gordon stopped Sandy and faced him. "It defends life's character as an agreeable enterprise."

"What are you trying to tell me, Gordon?"

"I'm saying trust your love, Sandy, even if it brings you heartache. Trust it, whomever or whatever its object; it will set you straight. Never let anyone or anything take from you your defiant will to love."

"I'll remember." Sandy started into the passage.

Gordon gripped his shoulder and stopped him again. "No, you won't. But I'm not talking to your mind, now, I'm talking to your heart and your spirit. When your memories return, you won't remember what happened here."

Sandy frowned.

"A great many people have come to see you."

"Who?"

"Your ancestors."

Chapter Twenty-eight

They entered a dark tunnel with walls of smoke. As Gordon and Sandy proceeded, the air acquired a red tint.

A voice called, "Who goes there?"

"Cumberland and Creaze," Gordon answered.

The haze cleared and a verdant expanse of rolling hills presented beneath a deep blue sky placid with artist's clouds.

At the foot of the nearest hill, a large gathering awaited. Gordon led Sandy to them. A man and a woman came forward to greet him.

"Hello, son," said the man, who wore coveralls and a workman's cap. "Sorry I wasn't there for you."

The woman embraced him. "I'm sorry I failed you, Sandy."

Sandy understood that these were his parents but he did not remember them. An older man in a suit and tie stepped up behind them. He embraced Sandy firmly and spoke quietly in his ear. "I know you still have the coin, Grandson. Spend it wisely."

Sandy was drawn on through the gathering. Some embraced him, some merely smiled. As he moved deeper into their midst he encountered many who were not human. Some had tentacles, some wings, some were insectoid, some humanoid with extra appendages or non-human visages. One was like a levitating globe with hundreds of radiating tendrils, with which it stroked Sandy's face affectionately.

"These are my ancestors?" Sandy asked Gordon.

"Some of them," Gordon said. "Not everyone could come."

At the end of the gathering stood a giant winged being Sandy had not noticed because its skin matched the coloration of the hill behind it. But then its scaly hide became brilliantly multi-hued.

Sandy stared up at the dragon in awe. "You're my ancestor?"

The dragon grinned and bent low to answer him. "When the time comes, you may remember *me.*"

Sandy stared about at the throng of his forebears, bewildered by the differences between them. They all bowed or bobbed to him, and he bowed to them in kind.

Gordon remained by his side. "It was good to see you again, Sandy."

"You too, Gordon. I wish I remembered you."

Gordon smiled. "You will, my friend. Now it is time for you to wake up."

"I'm not awake?"

Gordon shook his head. "This is a dream, dear boy."

"Oh."

"Give Appox my regards."

"Who?"

Gordon slapped Sandy hard and shouted, "Wake up!"

Chapter Twenty-nine

Sandy startled awake in a dim surround of dense, sickly vegetation. The damp ground he lay on had an unwholesome, slimy feel, and the air stank of rot.

Sandy stood up quickly and wiped what mud he could from his clothes. In the faint, sourceless light he noticed another unpleasant aspect of the place. Languishing in the mud were innumerable corpses and dismembered body parts.

He pulled out his map. The paper had turned black; the markings on it now showed in luminous white. It identified his location to be an indistinctly defined area called the Vile Swamp. An arrow pointed away from the direction Sandy faced, toward a structure some distance off identified as the Citadel of the Maimed.

He went the way the arrow pointed, pushing through thick, sagging foliage that had an oily texture. He breathed as shallowly as he could. Through mouth or nostrils the air was awful. His route was made serpentine by stinking pools filmed over with blackish-green scum. He found a muddy trail.

No stars or roof were apparent overhead. A gauzy webwork of luminous filaments, attached to nothing, here and there glimmered in the air. Sandy emerged from the cloying jungle and came in sight of the Citadel. It stood like a profane cathedral at the center of a putrescent bog blotched with feculent pools. Its walls and spires flowed with a black, leaden sludge.

Three men stood at the top of the stairs leading to the Citadel's entrance. The one on the right was tall and thin and wore a white straw hat; the one on the left was short and built like a wrestler. Both seemed familiar to Sandy, unpleasantly so. But the one in the middle, in a long black coat that glimmered faintly with many colors, held his attention. Sandy did not remember the man, but he experienced an intense dislike for him.

A name came to mind. "Garritch," Sandy said. He strode toward him.

"I must admit you are tenacious, Knight-errant," Garritch said.

Sandy didn't respond but he slowed his gait. Things were stirring in the ugly pools. Oily-black, humanoid figures rose from them, like sludgy mimicries of soldiers at attention. Sandy stopped and patted his pockets for something that wasn't there.

"No, no, no," Garritch said, "you've left your trinket behind. Even with your talisman you could not defeat my army. No one can. They are numberless and eternal."

The short man by Garritch cackled.

Sandy took in the horde arrayed against him. He could not defeat them. He looked at his map. It showed Garritch and his two human minions as red x's, and a host of white arrows coming toward Sandy, who had been reduced from an arrow to a white x. It showed him nothing he had not ascertained for himself: he was surrounded.

"Turn back now, Knight-errant, and I will spare you," Garritch said. "I have no desire to kill so entertaining an adversary."

Sandy had no intention of turning back. He couldn't remember why, but he knew that he had to deter Garritch from whatever he was doing.

Many of the ur-soldiers were armed with swords and lances. If he could disarm one, and take its weapon, he might be able to fight his way to Garritch. A soldier nearby on his left seemed the best candidate.

He was poised to make the attempt when a light from above bleached the landscape. A bright rectangle opened in the air to his right. A man stepped through and came toward him, as if descending invisible stairs. The man was tall, lean and dark-skinned, with a striking face. He smiled at Sandy and held out a vernier caliper.

"As I vowed, Alexander," he said.

Sandy took hold of the caliper and its power surged through him. His memories swept back to him, as if all the doors and windows of his mind flew open at once, and he knew himself again.

He extended his sword, donned his armor and faced Garritch. "Let's see how I do now, shall we?"

"You've chosen to die here, too, then, Appox?" Garritch said, the confidence in his tone less steady.

"I and a great many others, Garritch."

The bog surrounding the Citadel flooded with lights, and hosts of the Quick emerged from the firmament through apertures of myriad shapes and dimensions. As their numbers swelled, more ur-soldiers rose from the putrid pools to meet them, until two great armies confronted each other, well-matched.

Sandy surveyed the legion that had come to his aid and hoped he had not lured its members to their doom. He recognized among them archetypes who had previously stood against him. Crisis was there, on her levitating divan, clad now in armor and wielding a sword, and Giant Bill Grundy in his ten-gallon hat. The Quick of all colors and kinds, allied as dreamed of in fantasy, stood with him.

Virgin and Sam positioned themselves closest to Sandy. The three exchanged comradely looks, and turned their attention to Garritch.

"This doesn't need to happen," Sandy called to him. "We can end this between us, you and I."

Garritch surveyed those arrayed against him, all levity gone from his face. He turned to enter the Citadel. His two presumptive lieutenants started to follow him but he stopped them with a negating gesture and pointed back at the scene of impending battle. The tall one clearly was not happy with this turn of events, the short seemed indifferent. They both drew pistols from inside their jackets.

"Gadfly and Slick," Appox growled.

Sam glared at the short one. "*That's* the bastard."

The ur-soldiers began their advance.

"They are animations! They're not alive!" Sandy shouted. "Feel no remorse and show no mercy!"

The two armies fell upon each other, and the air filled with cries and the din of clashing steel and gunfire. The Quick were more effective than the ur, and at first pressed swiftly through their ranks. But more and more ur rose to replace the fallen, until both sides reached impasse, and held the ground they had.

Gadfly and Slick stayed behind the ur-soldiers, firing through gaps at the Quick. Their bullets were especially deadly, as they penetrated archetypal armor. Sandy saw Crisis go limp and her divan plunge into the bog. Appox managed to get a clear shot at Gadfly, and the tall man fell, his white hat tumbling. Sandy wielded his blade with unfettered rage, redoubling his efforts as he saw the ranks of the Quick diminish before the dead. His armor ran thick with the ichor of the lifeless.

It was not his objective to defeat this army. He summoned together a phalanx of fighters and they strove towards the entrance of the Citadel. But the ur were too many, and there was no end to them. Gradually the fight began to turn against the Quick. Even Bill Grundy was weakening. He had taken many bullets from Gadfly's gun.

A crack and a rumbling boom, like the mother of all thunders, reverberated down upon the bog, and the fighters on both sides were arrested. The atmosphere seemed to thicken, and an elusive noise, like crackling parchment and grinding steel, etched the air. The ur-soldiers lost cohesion and melted back into the pools from which they had risen.

A hazy figure coalesced near Sandy, as if assembling itself from the atmosphere. Sandy stared at the Hierophant, gladness for his intervention sullied with bitterness for the fallen.

Sandy glimpsed movement at the edge of vision, across the bog near the Citadel. Before he understood what was happening, Virgin leapt to shield him and a shot rang out. She slumped to the ground. Sandy saw Slick with his pistol aimed at him. The Hierophant flicked his hand, and Slick's gun flew from his grasp and spun off into the swamp.

Sam swept down and cradled Virgin in his arms. "No, no, darling, stay with me. You're okay, you're all right."

She caressed his face. "Sam."

"Appox!" Sam cried, "I need a doctor!"

Appox knelt beside Virgin. There was nothing to do. All the years the Labyrinth had taken from Beatrice Cloutier returned to her. It was heartbreaking to see her wither. Her chain mail transformed into a nun's habit and sandals. Sam held her frail remains.

Sandy whirled on the Hierophant. "You took your fucking time getting here!"

"I came when I could," Cabal said in his liquid voice.

Sandy hated the absence of feeling in that infant face.

Appox picked up his shotgun and stood from Virgin's side. "Which way did he go?"

"That way," Bill Grundy pointed across the marsh.

"He cannot quicken," Cabal said. "I have bound him."

Appox started after Slick.

"No!" Sam shouted. Gently, he lowered Virgin's body to the ground. He stood, looking down at her. "He's mine."

"I'll go with you," Sandy said.

Still gazing at Virgin, Sam shook his head. He gripped Sandy's shoulder. "You've got other business." He tilted his head back at the Citadel. "Give him my regards."

Sam stalked off after Slick. Appox, Bill Grundy, and several others followed him.

Sandy collapsed his armor and sword and pocketed his caliper. Many drew to him to accompany him into the Citadel.

"Only the Knight-errant can approach Garritch in his Citadel," Cabal told them, holding his hand up—gloved, this time, and masculine. "Even I would die if I attempted to accompany him."

"Thanks, everyone," Sandy said. "There's only one death I want today." He knelt by Virgin and kissed her pale brow. Her skin was thin as parchment. "Travel well, sister."

He stood and found the Hierophant watching him.

"Any useful counsel, Cabal? That you can express comprehensibly?"

"When you find him, remember your innermost self."

Sandy looked away, biting his lip. "I guess not." He zipped up his jacket and strode toward the Citadel.

CHAPTER THIRTY

A black, flowing ooze coated the walls inside Garritch's eldritch keep; mired within it, strips of flesh and disembodied faces slipped downward. The ooze extruded from a seam in the peak of the ceiling, into gutters covered with iron grates that bordered the floor of the entrance hall. The meatier components broke apart, passing through the grates.

Sconces bearing black candles lit the passage. Sandy ran toward tall oozing doors at the end. The floor looked like stone but was spongy underfoot. The softness increased as he went, until his feet sank into it, and he had to wrench them free with each step. He sank to his knees, drew his sword and hacked at the false stone to no avail. The black ooze welled up from the gutters, rising as he sank deeper. He saw that he could not escape, held his blade to his chest and stilled himself.

The ooze covered Sandy's head. Down and down he sank, like a stone through primordial muck. He let go of thinking and did not resist. Ethereal voices called his name, mocking him and enticing him to struggle.

He fell though the ooze into an immense white chamber with walls of bleached bones. He landed on the floor in a crouch, looked up to see the ceiling knit itself closed above him.

Sandy turned slowly. There was no sign of Garritch, nor any door. It was certainly a trap, but its nature was unclear.

The room was more than an ossuary. The bones fit together in some arcane way. They began to move, clicked and twisted and shifted among each other, forming gears and patterns with a purpose.

Sandy felt an elusive disruption inside of himself, affecting more than his body. His thought processes began to falter. The disruption went deeper than that, though, deeper than mind or physical being.

He was beyond any emotion that might strain his composure. He remembered how he had transcended pain, when the Hierophant placed the black feather in his palm. A more profound detachment was needed here. He had to step outside of his mind, the condition of consciousness that inhabited his body, and view it objectively to understand what was happening.

The bones clacked and clattered, twisted and turned. Bones were bones were bones, the support structure and refuse of life. His mind oscillated, vibrated, fragmented, the connections between memories shattered like glass.

But he was outside of that. He'd been so before; he didn't know when. He saw his mind as a coalescence of energy in a state of flux. The energy was tethered to his physical body, its temporary harbor—a clockworks of vim, viscera and perspective. That clock could run forward or back. It had an inception point and a terminus. The machine connected the two, meeting birth with death.

Birth linked death linked birth linked death, and the machine kept folding it over, more than a mind linked to a body could endure. Sandy watched his mind begin to collapse on itself, struggling to retain its human design.

Meanwhile he thought about bones. The bones with which the room was constructed and those of his own skeleton. He had made a long study of bones. One could view them as a history, and thus a path. A path which linked his bones with those of his ancestors.

There were many bones behind him. Fragments in piles, forgotten graveyards, paleontological periods … Bones linked souls as well as minds; they must if he had lived other lives, which somehow he knew that he had, though he could not remember them. His soul was and had been dependent upon bones to shore up the minds it had worn.

"When the time comes, you may remember me."

Sandy remembered Melchior's skeleton in Thracia's palace. Somewhere, in the lineage of his flesh, such a creature once had dwelt. He thought of the features of that skeleton, how the bones articulated, one to another, and in those linkages perceived a key to an invisible door.

He turned the key in the lock and opened the door.

His bones began to grow, and his flesh with them. He howled with the pain of transformation and submitted to it. His clothes shredded and fell away, his skin hardened with scales, his spine elongated and sent forth a long and powerful tail. He grew until his body almost filled the room. At the same time his mind gained dimension, sufficient to encompass its fragmentation, arrest and repair it. His mind grew greater than the bone engine.

Sandy studied the machine through his dragon eyes and identified its core. He bit into the wall, tore loose a chunk, spit it out with distaste, and peered into the cavity. The bones continued to shift and turn, compensating for the damage. He bit deeper, muzzling into the mechanism until he exposed its obscene heart, pulsing with *liquori mortem*. Sandy steeled himself and bit again, crushing the bone machine's heart.

Somewhere, Garritch screamed.

Sandy wretched and spat. He detected other ingredients in the *liqouri mortem*. It had been catalyzed with ectoplasm and the *rem viventum* of disintegrated souls.

He swung his mouth upward and vented his rage at the abomination in a torrent of fire, burning through the ceiling and the floor above it, unleashing conflagration until the entire Citadel was engulfed, until it was incinerated and all that remained was the smoldering rim of the chamber of bones.

A section of the bone wall fell open and Garritch slumped out on the floor.

Sandy loomed over him and rumbled, "Yield."

Garritch shrieked and curled up, shielding his head with his hands and frantically nodding submission.

Sandy's dragon self began to lose coherence. He relieved himself of millennia and diminished back into his human form, retrieved his vernier caliper and wallet from his shredded clothes, and collapsed on the floor beside Garritch. His desire to kill him was spent.

Garritch shrank from him.

"You looked so hard at death you blinded yourself," Sandy told him.

Whimpering, Garritch peeked timorously at Sandy.

"This whole side of the Labyrinth is one giant door, Garritch. You can't close *that.*"

Garritch stared up at the featureless sky, his eyes widening with horror as understanding struck.

"We can't see it because we fear the loss of loss." Sandy pulled himself to his feet and took a long breath. "And believe me the dead fear it too. Where's Lark?"

Garritch pointed a shaking finger toward the far end of the chamber. A door appeared in the bone wall and creaked open.

Chapter Thirty-one

Beyond the door, Sandy encountered a maze of transparent mirrors. He could see himself reflected on standing panels of thick glass, and could also see through himself, into a cosmos of stars and celestial events. Through five of the panels he saw Lark—five versions of her, malnourished and filthy in glass-enclosed chambers hardly larger than kennels, supplied only with narrow beds and meager facilities.

He was so stricken with disgust he wanted to look away. The Larks were all ensnared by gauzy filaments, and preoccupied with insipid pursuits. One was locked in an argument with herself, one in a state of denial, muttering "No" over and over, one was rapt in awe of some blissful vision, one in a morose state of resignation. Sandy stopped before a Lark immersed in an obsessive state of physical ecstasy. Garritch had beguiled her with sensual diversions, perverting the essence of who she was.

Sandy sheathed his hand in a gauntlet and smashed the glass, slashed the webs that held her with his sword. He gathered her in his arms. Sheltering her flesh restored his soul. She scowled and struggled, but then her eyes fluttered open and she saw him.

"I know you," she said

"But you do not remember me."

She blinked at him, confused.

"It will come back to you." He helped her to her feet and held her until she was steady, then took her hand and led her out of the cell.

He did not know what he was doing, had only intuition and caring to guide him. He signed the Lark of Love to wait, broke into the cell of the Lark of Trust, freed her and held her until she, too, came back to herself. Again her eyes fluttered open, and again she knew him but did not remember him. He led her out of her cell to the Lark of Love, drew them into a mutual embrace and closed his eyes. For awhile he held two women, then it were as if time and space folded over each other, like going to sleep in one country and waking in another to realize both were the same, and he held one.

After that she helped him. Together they freed her other aspects, tending last to the Lark of Respect, for she was in the most dejected state. They drew Lark together until all of her aspects were rejoined. Sandy shook out the cleanest blanket he could find and draped it around her shoulders.

He realized, as she looked at him, that he was seeing her for the first time, though that was both true and not.

Her tangled hair was reddish brown; in all other regards her appearance was the same, save she was gaunt from her ordeal. He understood how Garritch had debased her, exploiting her humanity against her, and again contemplated killing him.

"Where are we?" she asked.

"In the Mirror Labyrinth, in the realm of the dead."

Recognition at last sparked in her eyes. "Sandy."

He smiled. "Yes, my love." He saw the depth of age in her, the courage with which she held to life, sheltering child-like wonder in the marrow of her being, and he accepted all that she was and would be, knowing that however the predations of time afflicted her appearance, she would always be beautiful to him.

"I had to come here," she said.

"I know. And I had to follow."

She touched the scars on his face. "What have I done to you?"

"Saved my life."

"Oh, Sandy."

"No, no, my love; no, no."

Tears spilled from her eyes and they held each other.

"Take me away from here," he whispered in her ear.

She embraced him more tightly. "Your wish is my command."

◆

They stayed awhile in Crystalon, resting and healing. Althea tended to them, and the resentment Sandy felt toward the kindly Queen faded. He also spent time with Ben and Niralia, and learned more of the deeper ways of love. Ben discerned that Sandy had the ability to douse, and taught him how it was done.

Appox and Sam came to visit them, and the four spent long spells on a palace loggia, contemplating the beauties of Crystalon, taking ease in each other's company. Sam hid his grief, but it showed in the lines of his face, which had deepened. Appox talked about his plans to reopen the Archetypes Club. He had encountered many fledgling archetypes, and wanted them to have a place where they could be among their own.

When they were rested and healed, Lark and Sandy left Crystalon. They traveled together through the Labyrinth, and Lark showed him many wondrous sights. His favorite was the Cavern of Colours, where for millennia denizens of the Labyrinth had painted vast murals on cyclopean walls. Sandy learned that Lark had a mercurial streak, and loved her more for her moods. Many times he wanted to ask her to marry him, but a little voice in him told him not to, and this time he listened.

When they tired of travel they returned to their bedroom among the stars. And there, outside of time and circumstance, anchored to no geography but love, with the heavens dancing about them, they immersed themselves in bliss. During one such visit, Sandy knew they would not leave together. When they had loved and laughed and satisfied their passion, Lark said, "I have to go on."

"I know." Sandy was sad, but he had known the time would come, and was prepared for it.

"The door is finally open."

"I know. I opened it."

"Do you hate me?" she asked.

"I cannot imagine ever even mildly disliking you."

"Would you follow me, my knight?" She hid her fear but he saw it.

"Until time and times are done," he promised. He made a face and she laughed, and he wished for no better music.

They dressed and she stepped to the only pair of curtains still hanging from the firmament at the edge of their love nest.

"I don't know where I'm going," she said, peering out.

"I'll find you," he said.

She raised her hand, palm out, and he brushed his fingertips against hers.

And she was gone.

Sandy stood at the threshold, gazing into the unknown, his heart at once heavy and full.

The atmosphere thickened, and a noise like crackling parchment and grinding steel etched the air. "You seek to leave the Labyrinth, Alexander Creaze."

Sandy sighed. "Give a guy a minute, can't you?"

The Hierophant held out an infantile hand.

Sandy retrieved his wallet from the bedside table, but did not immediately relinquish his grandfather's coin. "You said I'd need another coin to go back to Earth. I'm not going back to Earth."

The Hierophant remained impassive with his hand extended.

Sandy grimaced. "I'm trying to convince myself you don't make this up as you go. Speaking of which, you expect me to believe you couldn't have handled Garritch?"

"I could not take the risk."

"Out of touch with your inner dragon?"

"I possess no such ancestor. If you had failed I would have tried." Cabal grinned his infantile, idiot grin.

Sandy eyed him skeptically. He placed the coin in Cabal's hand.

"Witness," Cabal said, while the coin began to heat. "Alexander Creaze, Knight-errant of the Unified Quints, Defender of the Traveling Doors, anointed archetype of the Earthly Continuum and Pilgrim of the Endless Plain, who ventures now to bear the human spirit unto the stars in pursuit of Love, I make to you this pledge. I, Cabal the Ageless, Hierophant of the Labyrinth of Souls, shall assume stewardship of the Five Doors, anchored in the realms of mystery and imagination by Lark Niamh Ó Cadhla. So long as I take breath, none who are not true to their aspects shall cross their thresholds, and this door shall remain ever open to you."

The coin finished absorbing into Cabal's hand. "Passage is granted, Alexander Creaze. You depart the Labyrinth by the Way of Discs."

"You're a weird cat, Cabal. I'm worried that I'm starting to like you."

Cabal's grin broadened.

Sandy gazed into the veils of stars. He looked at his map. The arrow stretched, arcing toward a pulsating image of a peony. He could not say for certain if Lark's love were true; he could not prove that it was, but it seemed true, and it felt true, and he could think of no better way to expend his life than find out.

About the Author

Stephen T. Vessels is a Thriller Award nominated author of Science Fiction, Fantasy, Horror, and cross-genre fiction. He wrote his first story when he was six years old, and forty years later wrote one that sold. Among his earliest inspirations were the horror films of Bela Lugosi, Boris Karloff and Vincent Price, SF films like Ib Melchior's "Journey to the Seventh Planet," and the legendary Modern Library anthology, *Great Tales of Terror and the Supernatural*, which he read in the back seat while his parents drove through Texas. In 2012 he received the Best Fiction award from the Santa Barbara Writers Conference. His first story collection, *The Mountain & The Vortex and Other Tales*, was released in 2016 by Muse Harbor Publishing. He is also a visual artist and his work has exhibited in New York and California.

He writes all of his drafts longhand. This is his first published novel.

stephentvessels.com

The Original

DUNGEON SOLITAIRE

Tomb of Four Kings

Still Available for Free

at

matthewlowes.com/games

Complete Rules
are Print-Ready and Playable
with any Standard Deck
of Playing Cards

Complete Rulebook
&
Labyrinth of Souls Tarot Deck
Available at
matthewlowes.com/games

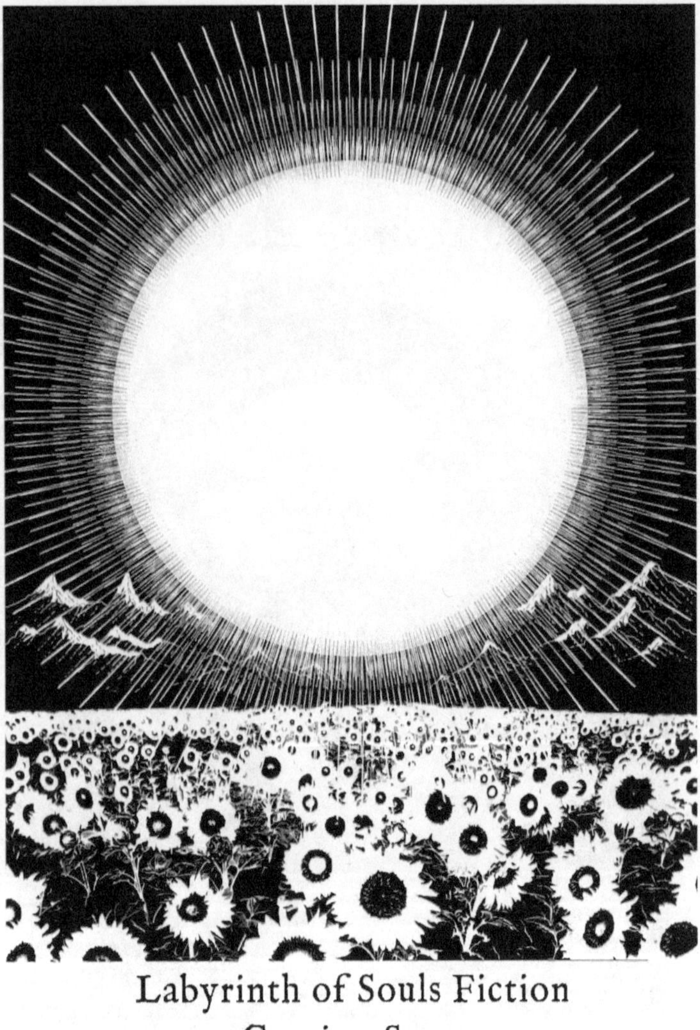

Labyrinth of Souls Fiction
Coming Soon

The Snake's Song by Mary E. Lowd
Mountain of Ashes by John Reed
Bayou's Lament by Cheryl Owen-Wilson
Perilous by Cynthia Coate-Ray

... and more to come!

information at
shadowspinnerspress.com

www.ingramcontent.com/pod-product-compliance
Lightning Source LLC
Chambersburg PA
CBHW020959120726
47905CB00009B/2768